PARABLE SEEDS

First Sowing

Jackson Day

PARABLE SEEDS

First Sowing

Jackson Day

PARABLE SEEDS:
First Sowing
©
Jackson Day

Copyright © 2011 by Jackson Day. Permission is granted to tell any of these crafted stories contained in this book, PARABLE SEEDS: FIRST SOWING, for non-commercial purposes, provided the storyteller gives the author credit for each story. Written permission is required for all commercial uses.

Cover prepared by Al Eiland

ISBN 978-0-9797324-4-7

http://biblestorytelling.org

OTHER BOOKS BY AUTHOR

- Old Testament Bible Stories   ISBN 978-0-9797324-0-9
- New Testament Bible Stories   ISBN 978-0-9797324-1-6
- Bible Storytelling Tools   ISBN 978-0-9797324-2-3
- Story Crafting   ISBN 978-0-9797324-3-0
- Quick Scripture Reference   ISBN 978-0-9797324-5-4
  for Life-Issues
- Outlines of Great Bible   ISBN 978-0-9797324-6-1
  Themes

CONTENTS

Acknowledgments. 1
Preface: Parable Seeds. 3
Bees Won. 15
Can't Undo the Past. 19
Child Did the Impossible. 23
Clothes Can Be Deceiving. 25
Cow's Bathroom. 27
Determined Baby. 29
Dog on the Thorn. 38
Enjoy the Coffee. 40
False Assumptions. 43
Giving Versus Sacrificing. 46
Giving While Living. 48
Greed – More Eggs. 50
Guitars. 53
Hidden Treasure. 58
Home Without a House. 64
Know Where You Belong. 66
Known by Friends. 69
Little Good Deed. 71
Lost Keys 74
Luck Isn't Talent 76
Most Important Thing. 78
Parachute Rigger. 82
Prideful Buck Deer. 91
Rabbit's Thesis. 94
Revenge Desires. 98
Soccer Daddy. 101
Traffic Camera. 109
Trash or Treasure. 111
Useless Nails. 114
Restricted Water Buffalo. 117
Weighed Down by Honor. 122
Wheat. 124

ACKNOWLEDGMENTS

I am a storyteller and I am a preacher who uses stories to communicate biblical teaching. Every time a listener talks to me about one of my stories, I'm inspired to keep telling stories.

My wife, Doris Emily Day, helps me as a storyteller and writer. When I first met her, I knew I had found a good looking woman who was fun to be around. I didn't realize she would become my partner in life. Sometimes she is behind me pushing me; sometimes she is by my side supporting me; sometimes she is in front leading me. I'm thankful for her help in preparing this book. If a good marriage is a sample of heaven, then I have been granted a foretaste of glory!

I'm challenged when it comes to grammar and spelling, and I have writer's blindness–I see what I think I wrote instead of what I actually wrote. I'm thankful for two friends who read the stories in this book, corrected mistakes, marked what was confusing and gave suggestions for improving them. They are:

- Mrs. Jennifer Farris is a stay at home mother with two young children. She is also a writer who finds life-lessons in everyday occurrences.
- Mrs. Diane Grill is a retired secretary with sharp eyes to spot spelling and grammar mistakes, and to spot words or phrases that could be misunderstood.

PREFACE: PARABLE SEEDS

Most people hear the word, "Parable," and think of the stories told by Jesus. Jesus captured the attention of his listeners with engaging stories that contained spiritual life-lessons. Jesus, the storyteller, attracted listeners as a magnet attracts iron. When Jesus spoke, all his listeners heard some good stories; spiritual, observant listeners heard a word from God.

The crafting and telling of parables began before Jesus and continues today. Parables and storytelling have continued within the Jewish and Christian communities. An important part of the Jewish community has been the maggids, who use storytelling to strengthen spiritual values and identity. The maggids are skilled narrators of the Torah and religious stories. Many teach through storytelling without explaining the stories told. For many centuries, two distinct classes of religious leaders in the Jewish community have been the scholarly rabbi and the storytelling maggid.

Most Aesop Fables are Jewish parables.

The mashal (meshalim - plural) is a type of Jewish biblical wisdom literature in the form of parables or proverbs. The Hebrew word *mashal* means, "It is like." Meshalim were classically used by rabbis to introduce a simile or parable to illustrate a point of teaching. A mashal can range in length from a few words to a long anecdote.

Throughout history, the Christian community has experienced preachers/teachers who have taught through storytelling, instead of interpreting the scriptures. They discovered and communicated biblical principles in everyday stories.

In the New Testament, Jesus never spoke without telling stories, called parables. The apostle Paul spoke and wrote using the philosophical discourse of the educated. Sometimes the philosophical, academic side of religion overshadows the storytelling side; and the interpretative, philosophical emphasis chokes out the storytelling role. When this happens, storytelling is positioned to a secondary inferior role. If the New Testament had a place for storytelling-Jesus and philosophical-Paul, the Christian church should value both storytelling and the interpretative-philosophical emphasis.

Christian academics tend to emphasize philosophical interpretation of the Bible and overlook storytelling to communicate biblical teachings. Christian academics may suppress storytelling, but will never kill it. Philosophical interpretation systems come and go, but great stories keep reappearing. It's like the kudzu vine in the deep South. The farmer may fight it and think it's gone, but it keeps reappearing and spreading.

Crafting parables to teach biblical principles has always been practiced by Christians with limited education. One seminary-trained pastor shared his story. Many Monday mornings, he phoned his father to talk about the sermon he had preached the previous day. Then his father would tell him stories. The pastor wondered, "Why can't I talk to my father about the truths I found in God's Word?" Finally, the pastor realized that his father, a man with a fifth grade education, was telling him stories that illustrated the truths the son had mentioned. Sometimes, his father would make up stories on the spot.

I had the joy of living in Brazil for thirty-three years. Storytelling is rooted in the Brazilian culture. I always carried 3X5 cards in my pocket. Whenever I heard a story I liked, I made notes on a card and threw it into a "story seed box." The majority of the stories/parables I tell were adapted from stories I discovered in Brazil.

A parable is one of the simplest of narratives. It sketches a setting, describes an action or event and shows the results. It is a short, fictitious story that illustrates a religious, spiritual or ethical situation. Often, it communicates a truth that could not be expressed in any other way but through a story, similar to the way music can express emotions that could never be portrayed through a speech. A parable, in story form, may simplify a complex teaching, allowing listeners to learn the complex concept via a short simple story.

I have a strong conviction that before we can change someone's beliefs, we must change the stories they hear and believe.

A parable is not a true story, but it communicates truth. A parable is a fictitious, concise story that illustrates how a person should behave or what they should believe. It has a moral or religious life-lesson and illustrates divine truth. It often involves a character facing a moral dilemma or making a questionable decision and then suffering the consequences.

A Christian parable is a fictitious story about ordinary men and women, in familiar settings of life, whose everyday experiences teach divine truth. A Christian parable is not about a giant of the faith; it is about a common person. It's a fictitious story, but it seems entirely probable.

A parable deals mainly with human affairs, but its overtone reaches into spiritual life-lessons. The defining characteristic of the parable is the presence of a prescriptive subtext that suggests a life-lesson about how people should behave or what they should believe. The subtext life-lesson is usually unspoken, but it is obvious to observant listeners. Parables are straightforward and obvious; they don't teach hidden or secret truths. Each parable has a point that the spiritually observant listener should understand. All listeners hear a good story, while the spiritually observant listener hears a word from God.

Parables are similar to fables because both generally relate to a single, simple, consistent action, without unnecessary detail or distracting circumstances. Both are short stories which are meant to illustrate a point or teach a lesson. A parable differs from a fable. Fables are about animals, plants, or inanimate objects that talk like people, while parables are about common people. A fable teaches a lesson called a moral. <u>A parable illustrates a life-lesson about how a person should behave or what they should believe</u>.

An ancient parable tells this story: Students were excited to receive a visit from a famous master-teacher. They expected the master-teacher to expound on deep intellectual truths. However, the teacher told one story after another.

A student requested, "Master, we want to hear you expound on profound philosophical subjects."

The master-teacher answered, "The older I get, the more I realize that the shortest road to guide people to the truth is to tell them a story."

Jesus told parables to put his listeners on the road to truth. I'm attempting to imitate Jesus by crafting stories that will put listeners on the road to truth.

WHY THE NAME, "PARABLE SEEDS"

The title of this book is "Parable Seeds." A seed needs to be planted and watered. It germinates and begins to grow. A tiny seed will grow into a larger plant. Then the gardener hoes around the sprouted plant to remove weeds that would choke it and prevent it from becoming a mature plant. A seed that germinates and matures will produce a harvest of many more seeds.

Each of the stories found in this book contains a seed of what you should believe or how you should behave. When you read or listen to these stories, allow these seeds to be planted in your own life. Take time to water them by thinking about the stories and searching to determine what the Bible says about the life-lesson revealed in the story. You may need to hoe around the sprouting plants by changing some of your thoughts or actions. My desire is that some of these seeds will germinate and grow inside you to produce a bountiful harvest.

Many times the storyteller can't tell if he is getting the message across to his listeners. The storyteller is similar to a DJ at a radio station. The DJ's station transmitter is sending out a signal. However, the DJ doesn't know to what frequency the receiver is tuned. In the same way, the storyteller is sending out a story; however, the teller doesn't know to what frequency the listener is tuned.

Jesus told a parable that may help the storyteller deal with this uncertainty. Jesus said, "The Kingdom of God is like this. A man scatters seed on the field. Both during the night when the man is asleep and during the day when he is awake, seed is sprouting and growing. The man doesn't understand how it grows. The soil produces the grain on its own accord– first the stalk, then the head, then the full kernel in the head. As soon as the grain is ripe, the man starts to reap because the harvest has come" (Mk 4:26-29).

Jesus told the parable to illustrate that the Kingdom of God will achieve its full development by virtue of its own hidden nature. But the parable also illustrates to me the nature of storytelling. The storyteller who narrates stories to communicate biblical teachings is like the farmer who scatters seeds. Stories have within themselves a life-giving nature capable of sprouting, growing and bearing fruit in the listeners' lives. The storyteller can't understand how it happens. The farmer plants seed every year without knowing if the weather is going to cooperate to make a bountiful crop. In the same way, the storyteller should keep telling stories even though he doesn't know if his listeners will cooperate to help the story grow. The storyteller's primary task is to tell the story. Then he can trust the story to sprout, grow and produce fruit, even though he doesn't understand how it will happen.

SUGGESTED WAYS TO USE THESE PARABLE SEEDS

Use Stories to Illustrate Biblical Truths

I became a pastor when I was twenty-six years old. I'm now seventy. I was a storytelling-preacher. Whenever I preached or taught, I always tried to illustrate every biblical teaching with a story.

I suggest that preachers and Bible teachers follow this principle: "Only teach or preach a biblical truth when you have a story to illustrate it."

If a teacher or preacher really understands something, no matter how complex it may be, he should be able to illustrate it with a story.

Use Stories to Communicate Truths That Are Hard to Swallow

When I was a child, the doctor prescribed for me a bottle of bitter medicine. After the first spoonful, I refused to open my mouth for Mother to give me another spoonful. She promised me cookies, then she threatened a spanking, but I refused to open my mouth for the bitter medicine. Mother mixed the bitter medicine into a glass of orange juice. I drank the medicine mixed with orange juice, but I wouldn't take the medicine by itself. There are biblical truths that are hard to swallow. If the truth is mixed into a story, it is easer to swallow. Often the naked truth is ugly and repulsive. However, when truth is clothed with a story, she becomes more attractive.

Use Stories to Communicate Truths While Entertaining

I retired from Christian ministry when I reached sixty-two years of age. I've recycled myself into becoming a storyteller. If someone asks me what I do, I don't tell them what I did in the past by saying, "I'm a retired missionary-pastor." I tell them what I'm doing, "I'm a storyteller." I feel honored when people introduce me as a professional storyteller. Often I tell stories to people I am meeting for the first time and will never see again. I joke to friends, "I tell lies on Saturday night and then go to church on Sunday and teach the truth."

Many people will listen to a storyteller who would never listen to a preacher. An organization invited me to do Bible storytelling training in Jacksonville, Florida. My host lived in a large apartment complex. My host sent invitations to the other residents of the complex to come to a Bible study on Wednesday night. Twelve people showed up. My host then sent invitations to the residents to gather around a campfire and hear a storyteller on Friday night. More than seventy-five people came to the storytelling event.

When I entertain as a storyteller, I usually start my gig by telling tall tales, change to telling folk or multi-cultural tales, and finish with parable seed stories. I've told many of the stories in this book on such occasions. My goal is that everyone be entertained with some good stories and that those who are spiritually sensitive hear a word from God. Usually, after a gig, a few people will approach me to talk about one of my parable seed stories. On one occasion a man told me, "When you told that story, I felt that God was speaking to me."

One storyteller told stories to campers around a camp fire. A teenager asked the storyteller, "How come I don't hear God speaking to me at church when they're talking about the Bible, but I heard him around the camp fire and you didn't mention the Bible?"

The New Testament values both storytelling-Jesus and philosophical-Paul. The Christian church should value both storytelling and the interpretative-philosophical emphasis. There are people who will never listen to the truth presented in interpretative-philosophical language, but they will accept the truth when it is clothed in a story.

From the casual storyteller telling tales to co-workers at a coffee break, to professional entertainers, we need Christians who tell stories that entertain their listeners, while giving a word from God to the spiritually sensitive.

Use Stories to Teach in Discussion Groups

I've used many of the stories in this book with a Bible study class and with a group where most listeners were recovering from drug or alcohol addiction. With both groups, I'd tell the story, then I'd ask the following questions to create discussion.

1. What life-lesson is illustrated by this story?
2. Does it illustrate a life-lesson that is true to Scripture?
3. What Scripture teaching does the story illustrate?
4. How should we apply this illustrated life-lesson to our lives?
5. Do we need to share the insight we received from this story with someone? Who?

I've found that telling a story and asking my listeners how it connects to the Bible is an excellent tool for teaching. I encourage you to try it.

Be Creative

I've given you some suggestions on how to use parable seeds. I encourage you to try them and to be creative and try things I've not mentioned. If you would, let me know your experiences. I could gain some ideas that I might share with others in how they could use Parable Seeds. The web site http://biblestorytelling.org will inform you how to e-mail me.

THE BEES WON

Tom and Ann Higgins loved camping. They went camping on their honeymoon. When camping, Tom set up camp, and then he cooked and washed the dishes with little help from Ann. Camping was vacation time for Ann. She took long walks and read while lying in a hammock. They went camping every summer for vacation and for each holiday weekend during the summer. A boy and a girl were born into the Higgins family and they grew up loving to camp.

Their son Dave was fourteen years old the year his father Tom died. Ann never thought about taking the children camping after Tom's death. Camping wouldn't be the same without her husband and their father.

The year Dave graduated from high school, his mother Ann told him, "I want to do something special for your high school graduation. I want it to be a memory-making occasion for you. What would you like to do this summer?"
Dave answered, "My happiest childhood memories are when we went camping as a family. Let's go camping again, like we use to with Daddy."

Ann didn't look forward to camping without Tom. It would be work and not a vacation. There would be little time to rest, take walks, and read. She would do the cooking and supervise her children doing the cleanup. Cooking on a camp stove on a picnic table would be more complicated than cooking at home in a modern kitchen.

The family went camping. They arrived at the campground that was so familiar to the family. Ann noticed the lake, trees, birds and flowers. She smelled the flowers. She heard the birds and gentle sound of lapping water. She began to grill hotdogs for supper and then she noticed the bees. A couple of bees constantly swarmed around her as she prepared hotdogs. Ann sprayed herself with bug spray and swatted at the bees, but they dodged her every swat. By the time the hotdogs were ready to eat at the picnic table, the two bees had sent for their family and five bees were swarming around.

That night, the bees sent out invitations for a family reunion. The next morning, Ann started preparing breakfast and more bees arrived. Still more arrived by the time eggs, bacon and biscuits were served on the table. By lunch time, the bees had invited their cousins, the flies, to come to the feast. One fly in particular kept landing on Ann's hair. Another would not leave alone the scab on her left leg. She swatted, they persisted, landing, bouncing, tickling, buzzing, and nibbling. Ann grabbed the fly swatter and spent ten minutes swatting at those two flies, but to no avail. The flies took off each time just before the swatter hit them. Ann kept interrupting her cooking to swat the bees and flies, and more kept arriving. Anger welled up within Ann. She called her children to eat, but Ann remained standing with a folded newspaper in one hand and a fly swatter in the other. She yelled and swatted at the bees and flies. Her fury seemed to beget more bees and flies.

Dave left the picnic table without eating, and sat under a tree. Ann followed her son and saw tears flowing down his cheeks. Her son sobbed, "Let's go home. My happiest childhood memories are when we went camping as a family. I wanted us to go camping one more time. I...I didn't realize how miserable you'd be camping without Daddy."

Ann realized, "The bees had won!" She wanted to give her son a memory-making week before he left home for college. But, the memories made were not the memories she wanted to give her son. The bees had won.

DISCUSSION

1. It is easy for the little things to sidetrack a person from achieving important goals.

2. Concentrating on lesser, irritating things will keep a person from experiencing the most important things.

CONNECTION TO THE BIBLE

Mt 13:7,22	Parable of the sower: Worries of life will choke out the Word of God.
Lk 9:57-62	Three men turned down the invitation to follow Jesus because of concerns for lesser things: One man wanted a bed to sleep in, another wanted to stay home until his father died, and another wanted a send-off party.
2 Cor 4:16-18	We do not lose heart. Fix eyes on the unseen, not on the seen; not the temporary but what is eternal.

CAN'T UNDO THE PAST

The pastor remembered the young lady who made an appointment to talk with him. He remembered when she was a student at the local high school. She had been head majorette of the marching band, the starlet of the high school play, and queen of the Senior Prom. She left home after graduating from high school and went west with dreams of becoming an actress or a singing idol. After several years of absence, she returned home. She retained her physical beauty, but the appearance of innocence had been replaced with hardness.

The young lady entered the pastor's study and told him her story. She made it as far west as Las Vegas. Sometimes she worked as a topless dancer. Most of the time she worked roulette tables. She drifted into prostitution after a man offered her five thousand dollars to spend one night with him. She averaged ten thousand dollars a week working as a prostitute. She enjoyed things money could buy, but bouts of depression appeared when she felt she had traded her body and soul for money. Time passed, depression increased, and enjoyment from spending money decreased.

The young lady asked the pastor, "How can I undo trading my body and soul for money?"

The pastor sat rubbing his chin. Then he said, "Your father recently planted some pecan trees. I want you to cut down one of those pecan trees; make a fire and burn it; gather up the ashes in a sack and bring the ashes to me."

The next day the young lady returned to the pastor's office with a plastic sack full of ashes.

The pastor told the young lady, "Now go back home and undo what you've done. Reassemble the ashes into the pecan tree."

The young lady said, "That's impossible! There's no way I can undo burning a tree!"

The pastor answered, "It's also impossible for you to undo your past. But in the present you can turn to God and receive his forgiveness, and in the future you can live a life that pleases him."

DISCUSSION

1. A person can't undo the past, but he can turn around his life in the present and change his actions in the future.

2. The Bible teaches that a person is saved from his sins by God's grace and not his own works.

CONNECTION TO THE BIBLE

Ps 32:1-5	God forgave David when he confessed his sins (2 Sam 12:13).
Ps 103:12	God removed the transgressions of the repentant sinner as far as the east is from the west.

Prov 28:13-14	The person who conceals his sins does not prosper, but whoever confesses and renounces them finds mercy.
Isa 1:18	God's invitation: Let us reason together; though your sins are like scarlet, they shall be as white as snow; though they are red as crimson, they shall be like wool.
Isa 55:6-7	Let the wicked forsake his way and the evil man his thoughts. Let him turn to the Lord, and he will have mercy on him; he will freely pardon.
Mt 6:12; Mk 3:28	Jesus taught us to pray for forgiveness.
Lk 7:36-50	Jesus forgave the prostitute who anointed his feet with perfume. He told her that her faith had saved her.
Jn 4:1-42	Jesus offered the Samaritan woman living water. She had experienced multiple marriages. She was used by God to convince her village that Jesus was the Messiah.
Jn 8:1-11	Jesus did not condemn the woman caught in adultery but told her to leave her life of sin.

Eph 2:8-10	A person is saved from his sins by God's grace, through faith in Jesus. He is not saved by his own works. But a person is saved to do good works.
1 Jn 1:9	If we confess our sins, God is faithful and just and will forgive us our sins and purify us from all unrighteousness.

CHILD DID THE IMPOSSIBLE

Southern old timers couldn't remember such a cold winter. Down South, it just never got close to 0 degrees. Farmers had never seen their ponds completely frozen over.

Children went to play on the frozen pond. One child ran to the middle of the frozen pond and jumped up and down. Suddenly, the ice cracked and the child fell into the pond. One of the children ran for help. Another ran to where his friend had fallen, and saw his friend under the ice fighting for breath. The child ran to the shore and returned with a rock. He pounded on the ice until he made a new hole for his friend. He held his friend's head above the frozen water until paramedics and firemen arrived and pulled the child out of the water. The paramedics put the shocked, trembling, and wet child into an ambulance.

The firemen asked the child who had helped his friend, "How did you pick up that rock? It's impossible! You're too small to carry that rock. You couldn't have held that rock in your hands to break the ice. Your hands are too small to hold that rock. It's impossible!"

The child's grandfather spoke up, "I'll tell you how he did it."

Everyone asked, "How?"

Grandfather answered, "There were no adults around to tell him it was impossible!"

DISCUSSION

1. A person should not take unnecessary chances.

2. There is more than one way to be a helper.

3. A determined person is often able to accomplish a task that others consider impossible.

CONNECTION TO THE BIBLE

1 Sam 17:33, 48-50	Saul told David that he, a boy, couldn't go against Goliath. But David defeated the giant.
Jn 6:9-10	A youth gave five loaves of bread and two fish to Jesus. Jesus used them to feed a multitude of 5000 men.
Mt 11:16	Jesus used children at play to illustrate spiritual truths.
Mt 18:2-4	Jesus used a child as an example. Childlike faith is essential to being Christ's follower.

CLOTHES CAN BE DECEIVING

A medical doctor's hobby was working with wood in his backyard workshop. One Saturday he was working in his shop when he received a call that paramedics were rushing an accident victim to the hospital. The doctor rushed to the hospital, still wearing faded, stained jeans.

The doctor treated the emergency. He was talking to the ambulance driver and a nurse when a well-dressed, distinguished looking lady arrived and asked, "Where can I find the doctor?"

The doctor replied, "Good afternoon. How can I help you?"

The woman sneered, "Are you deaf? Didn't you hear me ask you where I could find the doctor?"

The doctor calmly answered, "Good afternoon. I'm the doctor. How can I help you?"

The woman sneered, "You, a doctor? With those clothes?"

The doctor answered, "Excuse me. I thought you were looking for a doctor, not a well dressed man."

The lady answered, "Well, when you're dressed like that, you don't look like a doctor."

The doctor replied, "Yes, clothes can be deceiving. I saw you walking toward me with your elegant clothes and I thought, 'Here comes a distinguished well mannered lady.' Yes, clothes can be deceiving."

Clothes can be deceiving. Make sure to always dress yourself with consideration for others and with good manners.

DISCUSSION

1. Character, not clothes, makes the person.

2. Make sure to always dress yourself with consideration for others and with good manners.

3. Stereotyping people often leads to reaching wrong conclusions.

CONNECTION TO THE BIBLE

Prov 13:3	The person who controls his mouth protects his own life. A big mouth comes to ruin.
Mt 7:7	You will be judged in the same way as you judge others.
Many texts	Many rejected Jesus because he did not act like the Messiah they expected.
Rom 12:3	Do not have too high of an opinion of yourself.
Jam 2:1-4	Do not discriminate against a person because of clothes.
2 Cor 4:18	Fix eyes on the unseen, not on the seen; not the temporary, but what is eternal.

COW'S BATHROOM

My wife and I spent thirty-three years in Brazil. Our children grew up in Brazil. My wife and I tried to do fun activities with them every week. We often went on picnics. On one occasion, Tim was three years old, John was eight, and Sam was ten. We took our sons to a lake to have a picnic and for me to take the two older sons fishing. I drove the car through cow pastures to reach the lake. The lake was in the middle of a cow pasture.

I took Sam and John fishing while three year old Tim stayed with his mother under a tree. She prepared a picnic and roasted hotdogs over an open fire. Three year old Tim wandered around the picnic area. Doris kept telling him, "Watch out! Don't step where the cows went to the bathroom. Tim, look at the ground. You're about to step where the cows went to the bathroom. Watch where you're walking! You don't want to step where the cows went to the bathroom."

The next day friends asked the boys, "Where did you go on your picnic?"

Sam and John answered, "We went fishing in a lake on a big farm."

Tim answered, "We went to the cow's bathroom."

DISCUSSION

1. A person will observe where he focuses his attention.

2. Where one person focuses on beauty, the other will focus on ugliness.

CONNECTION TO THE BIBLE

Mt 6:22-23	Good eyes see light; bad eyes see darkness.
Rom 12:2	Be transformed by the renewing of your minds.
2 Cor 4:18	Fix eyes on the unseen, not on the seen; not the temporary, but what is eternal.

DETERMINED BABY

Every year, Helen said, "The best thing about Christmas is being with family. Christmas without family wouldn't feel like Christmas." But in 2010, she was unable to spend Christmas Day with her family.

Helen grew up in Kentucky in a spacious home on the backwaters of Kentucky Lake. Her parents' home was the gathering place for all family reunions that took place every Easter, every Mother's Day, every Father's Day, every July 4th, every Thanksgiving, every Christmas, and most Sundays. Helen studied to become a registered nurse at Western Kentucky University in Bowling Green. Every weekend and every holiday, she made the 100 mile drive back to her parents' home on the lake. Helen graduated from nursing school and got a job as a nurse at Lake City, the closest town to her parents' home. She was overjoyed to again live in her parents' home on the backwaters.

One morning Helen was fishing off the dock behind her parents' home. She asked a man who was casting from a nearby boat if he was having any luck. The man replied, "Haven't caught any fish, but hope my luck is changing." He introduced himself as Bill and asked Helen to go fishing with him the next weekend. The rest is history. Bill and Helen married and lived in a mobile home on the same lake as her parents. They ate dinner at Helen's parents' home every Sunday. Every holiday was spent at Helen's parents' home. Bill and Helen had every intention of living out their lives on Kentucky Lake.

However, Bill lost his job and could not find a job close to their home. Bill had been unemployed for six months when he found a job at the new Kia Plant in West Point, Georgia. Helen got a job at East Alabama Medical Center in Opelika, Alabama. She worked weekdays from 7:00 a.m. to 3:00 p.m. Every three months she was required to work a weekend.

Bill and Helen bought a home in town. On Sundays, Helen was always homesick for Sunday dinner at her parents' home. Helen and Bill traveled the 450 mile trip to her parents' home for every major holiday. Bill and Helen had a one year old baby named Adam and a six year old daughter named Christy.

In 2010, Christmas fell on a Saturday. Helen's supervisor told her she was scheduled to work on Christmas weekend. Helen argued, "The best thing about Christmas is being with family. Christmas won't feel like Christmas if I can't be with my family." Tears and pleadings didn't change the supervisor's mind. It was her time to work the weekend. No one was willing to swap out with her. The other nurses wanted to spend Christmas with their families. This would be the first Christmas that Helen wouldn't be at her parents' home. Bill and Helen did go to Kentucky Lake the week before

Christmas. But they had to leave her parents' home after lunch on Christmas Eve so Helen could go to work on Christmas Day.

Helen was teary-eyed when she, Bill, one year old Adam and six year old Christy got in the car and drove away from her parents' home. As Bill drove down Interstate 24 and then 65, Helen kept complaining, "The best thing about Christmas is being with family. Christmas without family won't be Christmas."

Few cars were on the interstate as they traveled through Kentucky, Tennessee, and into Alabama. After it got dark, six year old Christy wanted to stop to eat. Twice, they got off Interstate 65 to follow a sign to a restaurant. Both times, they discovered the restaurants were closed so employees could spend Christmas Eve with their families. Their third stop was close to Decatur, Alabama. The restaurant was open. Two cars were parked by the side of the restaurant. An old flatbed truck stacked with crushed cars from some junkyard was the only vehicle in front. The truck looked like an escapee from a junkyard.

The restaurant was empty except for a cook, a waitress and a middle-aged man, the driver of the old truck. He looked as much a wreck as the wrecked cars he was hauling. He smelled of filth and beer. His coat was dirty, greasy and torn. His baggy pants were covered with grease and stained with rust. His work boots were stained with grease and dried mud. He held a bottle of beer in his hand. Two empties sat on the table in front of him. His gums had as few teeth as baby Adam's.

The truck driver didn't look up as Bill, Helen, and their children, passed by his table. Baby Adam shouted, "Hi." The man gave a quick stare at the one year old, then bowed his head to stare at empty beer bottles on the table. Helen wanted to leave, but Christy said, "I'm hungry, I wanna eat." Bill said if they didn't eat there, he had no idea where they would find another open restaurant. Bill sat closest to the truck driver. Adam was in a metal high chair between Bill and Helen.

Adam squealed with glee and pounded his baby hands–paw, paw, paaaw–on the metal high chair. Then he swayed back and forth, ducking behind his father, raising quickly and squealing with delight. He wriggled and giggled. Helen saw that baby Adam was playing peek-a-boo with the truck driver. The truck driver looked at baby Adam with sad eyes. Bill kept telling Adam, "Quiet down!" Helen gave her "Shush-sssheee." She tried to get Adam's attention. Christy said, "Adam is embarrassing me." But Adam only had eyes for the truck driver.

The waitress served the family. Baby Adam kept up his banging, squealing and playing peek-a-boo with the truck driver. The truck driver looked at Adam with the beginning of a smile. Then he picked up a menu and began to play peek-a-boo with baby

Adam. Adam ducked behind his father to hide from the truck driver, then he quickly raised up so he could see the truck driver. He squealed with delight and banged on the metal chair – paw-paw-pa-pa-paaaw.

The truck driver shouted, "Why, you wanna play peek-a-boo. Ha, ha. You know peek-a-boo. How about that! Peek-a-boo."

Adam would squeal "Hi" and the truck driver would respond with a loud, "Peek-a-boo. How about that?"

Christy asked, "Why is that dirty old man so loud?"

Bill and Helen were frustrated with Adam. They couldn't get his attention. He only had eyes for the truck driver.

They finished eating. Bill got up to pay the bill. Helen took baby Adam in one arm and used her other hand to hold on to Christy. They moved past the truck driver's table and Helen held her breath to avoid the smell of filth and beer. Adam leaned over and stretched out both arms in a baby's pick-me-up position. Then, in a split second, baby Adam lunged for the truck driver. If the man hadn't caught Adam, the baby would have fallen to the floor.

The man asked, "Can I hold your baby?"

Before Helen could answer, Adam propelled his arms around the man's neck. Adam lay his tiny head on the greasy coat that covered unwashed shoulders. The man closed his eyes; tears ran down his cheeks. Calloused, greasy, unwashed hands gently stroked the baby's back.

The man opened his eyes, looked squarely at Helen and said, "Give this baby plenty of love. You hear me?"
Helen had a knot in her throat and could only murmur a soft, "OK."
The man reluctantly, yet lovingly, pried baby Adam from his chest. Adam tried to cling to the man's neck. Helen held her arms open to receive her baby. The half-drunken truck driver said, "Merry Christmas, Ma'am. Merry Christmas. You done give me my Christmas gift."

Tears ran down Helen's face as she held Adam in one arm and with the other grasped little Christy's hand. She led Christy out to the car.

In the car, Helen and Bill got to talking about the fact that the way Adam embarrassed his family was similar to the way Jesus embarrassed those around him. Adam, like Jesus, was determined to reach out to an individual that others wished he would ignore.

Jesus has God's arms, zeal and passion to embrace wrecked lives with wrecked relationships. Jesus has two arms determined to embrace those who are outcast because of choices they have made. Christmas is about Jesus' fierce desire to embrace people we wish he would ignore.

Sweet little baby Jesus, we wanna hold you in our arms. But, sweet little baby Jesus, you embarrass us; you reach out to embrace people whom we wish you would ignore.

Those who have not allowed Jesus to embrace their wrecked lives have no reason to celebrate Christmas. Those who have not allowed Jesus to embrace their wrecked lives can celebrate the winter holiday season, party, give gifts and receive gifts. But they have no reason to celebrate Christmas, the birth of baby Jesus. But we who have allowed Jesus to embrace our wrecked lives have reason to celebrate Christmas. We have reason to celebrate the birth of Jesus. We have reason to joyfully shout the greeting, "Merry Christmas." We who have allowed Jesus to embrace our wrecked lives should be like Jesus this Christmas; we should reach out to embrace those with wrecked lives who often are ignored by others.

Sweet little baby Jesus, we wanna hold you in our arms. But sweet little baby Jesus, you embarrass us; you reach out to embrace people whom we wish you would ignore.

It started the night of his birth. Shepherds were outcasts. Centuries ago, honorable men such as Abraham and David had been shepherds. By the time Jesus was born, shepherds had become hired hands who would not risk themselves to protect other people's sheep. They were undependable. In fact, shepherds were considered so undependable that a shepherd couldn't testify in court. Shepherds were stereotyped as undependable liars. Yet, shepherds were the first visitors who came to see baby Jesus.

Sweet little baby Jesus, we wanna hold you in our arms. But sweet little baby Jesus, you embarrass us; you reach out to embrace people who we wish you would ignore.

Baby Jesus, on the night you were born, why didn't you reach out to embrace leaders of the local synagogue, or priests from the Temple? Why did you reach out to embrace such notorious liars? Nobody would believe their story.

DISCUSSION

1. Who are some people with wrecked lives who Jesus embraced, but others wished he had ignored?

2. How has Jesus embraced you with your wrecked life?

3. Are there types of people with wrecked lives who you wish Jesus would not embrace?

4. Allow yourself to be the arms of Jesus. Reach out to embrace someone with a wrecked life who is ignored by others.

CONNECTION TO THE BIBLE

Jn 4	Jesus offered 'living water' to the Samaritan woman who was a home-wrecker.
Lk 4:14-30	Jesus was rejected in Nazareth when he described how in the past, non-Jewish foreigners received blessings from God that were not given to Israelites.
Lk 5:27-32	Jesus chose the tax collector Matthew to be one of his disciples, and went to his home to eat. Matthew worked for the foreign oppressor. Fellow Jews considered him traitorous and dishonest.
Lk 7:36-50	Jesus allowed a prostitute to touch him, and he forgave her. She had sold pleasures that wrecked other people's lives. This offended the Pharisees.
Lk 10:30-37	Jesus made the hero of his story a Samaritan who belonged to a race that was despised by fellow Jews.
Lk 15:1-24	Jesus was accused of eating and drinking with sinners and social outcasts. Jesus told three stories about things lost and found, and emphasized that Heaven rejoices when a lost sinner is found.

DOG ON THE THORN

A visitor dropped by the home of a farmer. The two men sat on the front porch visiting. As the two men visited, they told stories. The visitor noticed a hound dog lying under the shade of a bush, whining and groaning with pain.

The visitor asked the farmer, "What's wrong with your dog?"

The farmer answered, "He's lying on the thorns of a rose bush."

The visitor asked, "Well, why doesn't he move?"

The farmer answered, "He's hurting enough to complain, but the pain isn't severe enough to make him get up and move."

DISCUSSION

1. Some people complain about problems they could easily resolve.

2. Problems continue when they are not faced and dealt with.

CONNECTION TO THE BIBLE

| Jos 23:5-13 | Joshua warned the Israelites that if they did not drive out the people of the land, those people would create problems for the Israelites. |

Prov 6:6	The lazy person should learn from the ant.
2 Thes 3:6, 10	Do not feed the person who will not work.

ENJOY THE COFFEE

An elderly gentleman was the key speaker at a spiritual retreat for young married couples. The young couples were already established in their careers. They had all bought their first house; they all had children at home.

The speaker led a study on being content with your situation in life. Several people told him it was a powerful study. It was something they needed to hear.

After the study, everyone went to the game room to play ping pong, pool, card games, checkers, chess, and to have fellowship. The speaker observed that the conversation soon turned into complaints about the cost of living, stress at work, disagreements with their children's teachers, co-workers getting promoted before them, and life in general.

The speaker made a large pot of coffee. He then set out a tray with different kinds of cups: paper, porcelain, plastic, glass, and crystal. Some plain looking, some expensive, some exquisite. The speaker called out, "Coffee is on; help yourself; enjoy the coffee."

After everyone had a cup of coffee in hand, the speaker called out, "May I have your attention. I noticed that the first in line took the best looking expensive cups, leaving behind the plain and cheap ones. It's normal for you to want the best for yourselves, but that's the source of your complaining. The cup doesn't affect the taste or quality of the coffee. In most cases the expensive cups even hide the coffee. What each of you wanted was coffee, not the cup; however, each of you sought the best cup available. Those of you who were left with the plastic or plain cups began eyeing those with better looking cups.

"Think about this: Life is like coffee; the jobs you have, the looks and talents of your children, the money you have or don't have, and your position in society are cups that help hold your life. The kind of cup you drink from neither defines nor changes the quality of your life. If you concentrate on the cup, you won't enjoy the coffee God has provided for you.

"God brews the best coffee for you, even if he doesn't give you the most impressive cup. Enjoy your coffee! Enjoy the coffee instead of complaining about the cup."

DISCUSSION

1. Often understood life-lessons are not put into practice.

2. The person who is thankful and content with his situation in life is truly blessed.

CONNECTION TO THE BIBLE

Prov 15:16	Better a little with the fear of the Lord than treasures with trouble.
1 Tim 6:6-8	Godliness with contentment is great gain. Be content if you have food and clothing.
Phil 4:12-13	Paul testified that he had learned to be content in any situation. He could face any situation with the strength Christ gave him.
Heb 13:5	Be content with what you have.

FALSE ASSUMPTIONS

Mr. Farmer remained on the family farm while the rest of his high school graduating class left the rural community for university or the military. After that they moved on to large towns or cities.

One day Mr. Farmer received a visitor. A former high school classmate dropped by to see him. Mr. Farmer opened his front door. There stood his high school friend with a large Labrador Retriever dog standing by his side.

Mr. Farmer greeted his friend, "It's been a long time!"
His former high school friend replied, "Yes, it's been a long time."

The Labrador Retriever took advantage of the greeting to enter Mr. Farmer's house. Mr. Farmer frowned. He didn't allow dogs in his house, but didn't want to offend his friend.

The two friends entered the living room and sat down to talk. Mr. Farmer stared as the dog wandered from the living room to the hallway. His visitor didn't seem to notice.
Mr. Farmer said, "Last time I saw you was at our high school's ten year reunion. What are you doing now? How's life treating you?"

Before the visitor answered, Mr. Farmer heard his wife give a shout from the kitchen, and then the ruckus of pots and pans falling. Mr. Farmer gritted his teeth, but his visitor calmly answered, "Life's been good to me. Got a good wife and a good job. One kid is in high school, the other is in college. How are things going with you?"

Before Mr. Farmer answered, he heard his wife shout, "Get off the bed." But his visitor was nonchalant. Mr. Farmer answered, "You know how it is for the farmer. Prices of fuel, fertilizer, and seeds gone up. Price of the crops gone down. Kinda dry this year. Don't know if I'm gonna break even this year."

The Labrador Retriever trotted into the living room, jumped over a table, knocked over a lamp, then jumped up on the couch and laid his head in the visitor's lap. Mr. Farmer let out a loud sigh, but his visitor pretended not to notice. The visitor felt tension in the air. He dismissed himself with, "Came home for the holiday, but wanted to drop by and see you."

As the visitor walked out the door, Mr. Farmer stated, "Call your dog. You don't want to leave him."

The visitor answered, "My dog? That's not my dog. When I arrived, the dog came to the door like he belonged here. Naturally, I thought he was your dog. You opened the door and the dog entered like he was at home. I thought he was your dog."

DISCUSSION

1. Things are not always as they appear.

2. The person who gets his exercise jumping to conclusions may reach the wrong conclusion.

3. Misunderstandings result when an obvious problem is ignored and not discussed.

CONNECTION TO THE BIBLE

Jos 22:1-34	The confusion about why the Eastern Tribes built an altar was cleared up with conversation.
Lk 5:17-26; 5:27-31; 7:36-50	On three occasions, Jesus knew the critical thoughts religious leaders had about him. Each time, Jesus brought the issue out into the open by speaking about it.

GIVING VERSUS SACRIFICING

The rural area of the Deep South was going through a severe recession. Many who had worked in the local mills had been laid off work and were facing hard times. Most were behind on house and car payments. Some had received letters from the bank threatening to foreclose on the house and repossess the car. Some were having a hard time putting food on the table for their children.

Cow, Chicken and Pig were in the barnyard. They heard Mr. Farmer and his wife talking about the dire situations of some of their neighbors during the economic hard times. Mr. Farmer suggested to his wife that they take vegetables from their garden to help friends who were going through hard times.

Cow told Chicken and Pig, "We also need to give something to help the needy."
Pig asked, "How we gonna help?"
Cow said, "I'll give milk.
Chicken said, "I'll give eggs."
Pig asked, "What can I give?"
Cow answered, "You can give bacon and ham."
Pig replied, "Not so fast. You two are just offering some help, but you're expecting me to sacrifice everything."

DISCUSSION

1. Do not challenge others to do more than you are willing to do.

2. A partial commitment demands far less than a total commitment.

CONNECTION TO THE BIBLE

Mt 23:1-12	Jesus criticized the scribes and the Pharisees because they didn't practice what they preached. They gave people heavy loads to carry, and would not help the people carry them.
Jn 13:15	Jesus set an example for what he wanted his disciples to do.
1 Cor 11:1	Paul challenged the Corinthians to follow his example as he followed the example of Jesus Christ.
Phil 3:17	Paul challenged the Philippians to follow his example and to observe others who followed it.

GIVING WHILE LIVING

A wealthy man complained that his generosity wasn't appreciated. He said, "My Last Will and Testament establishes a foundation to administer my wealth. My wealth is gonna do a lot of good. My foundation will add a new wing to the children's hospital. My foundation will build a new science lab at the local university. My foundation will build and maintain a continuing educational technical school to train unemployed and under-employed adults."

One of his listeners replied with a story:

One day Pig and Cow were talking. Pig complained, "It's not fair. You get more respect on the farm than I do. My bristles will be used to make brushes for artists. My pigskin will be used to make shoes, purses and gloves. People will eat my bacon, ham, and pork. Everyone says that the best barbecue is barbecue pork."

Cow answered, "I get more respect than you because I give milk every day; you only give after you die."

DISCUSSION

1. Good deeds should be done while one is alive, and not postponed until after death.

CONNECTION TO THE BIBLE

Lk 12:19	Confidence in wealth leads a person to be presumptuous.
Jn 11:9	Jesus said that one should take advantage of the twelve hours of daylight.
1 Tim 6:6-10	Godliness with contentment is great gain. Be content with food and clothing. Love of money is the root of all kinds of evil.

GREED – MORE EGGS

Mrs. Farmer wanted some spending money. Mr. Farmer suggested, "You've got a dozen hens that are laying eggs. Each lays an egg a day. You aren't using most of the eggs. Sell the extra eggs and keep the money for your spending money."

Mrs. Farmer started gathering the eggs each morning and selling them to the town-folks. The town-folks liked her farm-fresh eggs better than the store-bought eggs. Mrs. Farmer noticed that each hen was laying an egg a day. She appreciated the extra spending money. Then she got to thinking, "If my hens laid more eggs, I'd have more spending money. I know what I'll do. I'll feed the hens twice as much chicken feed. Then I'll collect twice as many eggs from the hens. I'll collect from each hen an egg each morning and another egg each night."

Mrs. Farmer put her plan into action. She started feeding the hens a double portion of chicken feed. The hens became fat and lazy, and stopped laying eggs.

Mrs. Farmer sold the fat hens to the town-folks. The following weeks, several families enjoyed fried chicken or barbeque chicken. By the time Mrs. Farmer paid the feed bill, she had lost money on her hens.

DISCUSSION

1. Seeking to satisfy greed results in unsatisfactory endings.

2. The greedy person seldom gets what he wants.

CONNECTION TO THE BIBLE

Gen 13:10-13	Lot was greedy and chose the fertile Jordan Valley.
Jos 7:13	Achan was greedy and took forbidden gold and silver from the spoils of Jericho.
1 Kin 21:2-16	Ahab was greedy for Naboth's vineyard.
2 Sam 11:1-5	David was greedy in wanting sex with Bathsheba, Uriah's wife. The result was discord in his own family.
1 Kin 12:1-17	King Rehoboam inherited the kingdom from his father Solomon. It was the richest kingdom in the world. Rehoboam wanted more, resulting in 10 of the 12 tribes abandoning him.
Lk 15:11-24	The prodigal son wanted his inheritance and ended up in the pig pen.
Jn 6:26	Greedy people wanted to follow Jesus just to eat loaves and fish.

Mt 19:6-22	The rich young ruler's greed for things kept him from following Jesus.
Lk 12:15-21	The rich fool forgot God and concentrated on material things to meet his needs.
Jn 12:4-6; Mt 26:14-16	Judas was greedy and betrayed Jesus for 30 silver coins.

GUITARS

The four Benton cousins grew up together close to Benton Crossroads. They were playmates in the sandbox as children. They attended the same school and played basketball and baseball together. They formed a country music band that played at school events, local talent shows and for local church functions. The band broke up when the oldest cousin graduated from high school and went off to college. In fact, two of the cousins went to college, one entered the Army and the other stayed home to work Grandfather Benton's farm. The musical instruments that were used by the band ended up in Grandfather Benton's attic.

The Benton cousins were nearly thirty years old when an aunt organized a Benton family get together to celebrate Grandfather Benton's eightieth birthday. The aunt who was organizing the event insisted the Benton cousins play and sing for the family reunion.

The cousin who had become Farmer Benton removed the musical instruments from Grandfather's attic to tune them before the other cousins arrived. He used a damp cloth to wipe the keyboard and guitar cases. He dusted off the keyboard. He planned to use the keyboard to get a clear, loud pitch to help him tune the guitars. He picked up the first guitar and plucked the sixth string, the low E string. Then he played the low E note on the keyboard. He tightened the tuning key to increase the tension on the E string until it reached the desired tone. The guitar screamed, "No! No! Please stop. You are hurting me. Why are you causing me such pain?"

Farmer Benton then tuned each of the other strings, going from the low notes to the high: E A D G B E. Each time he turned the tuning key to increase the tension on a string, the guitar moaned and groaned.

When Farmer Benton was satisfied with the first guitar, he put it down and picked up the second guitar. He tuned the second guitar. It moaned and groaned each time Farmer Benton turned the tuning key to increase the tension on a string. As soon as he played a song, the guitar went out of tune. Farmer Benton realized that the old strings had become flattened where they contacted the fret wire. They sounded dull, and it would be impossible to keep the guitar in tune with those strings. Farmer Benton turned the tuning key to release the tension on the strings, then he picked up a pair of wire cutters and started cutting the strings. The guitar screamed, "No! No! Please, no surgery. Don't take my strings away. I don't want to give up my strings. I've had them all my life."

Farmer Benton replaced the strings. The guitar resented reconstructive surgery as strange strings were attached to her. Farmer Benton tightened each tuning key to increase the tension on each string. Then he stretched each string by pulling it away from the guitar's body and releasing it so the string struck and strung the neck of the guitar. The guitar screamed, "This therapy is torture! This man is a torturer. He loves to inflict pain on me."

Farmer Benton picked up the third guitar, an Archtop Acoustic Guitar with steel strings. The guitar screamed with pain as Farmer Benton tightened the tuning key for each string to get it tuned up.

The fourth guitar, a Martin Acoustic Guitar had been placed on the floor at the end of the couch. Martin Guitar began to pray, "Lord, protect me. Save me from the torture that my fellow guitars have suffered. I'll do anything you want if you will just save me from this suffering."

Apparently, Martin Guitar's prayers were answered. Out of sight; out of mind. Farmer Benton didn't see Martin Guitar lying on the floor at the end of the couch. Martin Guitar prayed, "Oh, thank you, Lord, for sparing me from suffering and torment. Oh Lord, you've revealed your goodness by protecting me from the tuning torment."

The day of the family reunion arrived. The four Benton cousins got together in the morning to rehearse with the guitars. Three of the cousins came together. Each picked up one of the guitars that had been tuned. They strummed the strings and experimented with different tunes. They exclaimed, "These sound fantastic!"

The fourth cousin finally arrived. He picked up Martin Guitar, who had escaped the tuning torture. When the cousin strung Martin Guitar's strings, a sound came out that was more irritating than the sound of fingernails scratching on a chalkboard. The cousin exclaimed, "What a horrible sound! This guitar is useless, at least until it's tuned. I'll use the keyboard."

The Benton cousins took the three tuned guitars and the keyboard to the family reunion; they left Martin Guitar abandoned on the floor. Poor Martin Guitar felt alone and started crying, "Nobody wants me. I escaped the painful tuning process, but I'm useless. They can't use me. I'm an outcast."

DISCUSSION

1. Suffering can become a tuning key that enables a person to make music.

2. Coaches often tell athletes, "No pain; no gain." How can life-inflicting pain produce gain for us?

3. How can people experience gain from suffering caused by evil people (murderers, thieves, sexual perverts, abusive people, bullies, addicts, etc.)?

4. Identify the "tuning keys" of our lives, and express gratitude for them.

5. Farmer Benton used the keyboard as the standard to tune the guitars. What are you using as a standard to tune your life?

6. Many prayer requests, if answered, would bring undesirable results.

CONNECTION TO THE BIBLE

Gen 50:20	Joseph told his brothers that their evil intentions had been used by God to bring about good.
Mt 5:10-12	Rejoice and be glad when you are persecuted for doing right.
Mt 16:21-23	Peter protested against the idea of Jesus suffering. Jesus accused Peter of thinking and talking like Satan.
Mt 26:36-46	Jesus suffered in the Garden of Gethsemane.
Jn 15:1-2	God prunes the branches that don't give fruit.
Rom 8:16-18	Share in Christ's suffering; share in his glory. Present suffering can't compare to future glory.
Jam 1:2-4	Consider it a joy when forced to face trials.
1 Pet 2:19-21; 4:12-13; 5:10	Sharing in Christ's suffering will result in rejoicing with Christ.

HIDDEN TREASURE

Two young ladies visited a church close to a university shortly after the school year began. They introduced themselves to the pastor as Jean and Jane Sanders. The pastor said, "I can tell you're sisters. Are you twins?"

Jean answered, "We're not sisters. We're first cousins."

Jane interrupted, "Our fathers are brothers. We grew up next door to one another, and we're closer than any sisters we know."

Jean explained, "We're first year students at the university. We live together in a small apartment."

The pastor gave his card to the cousins and told them to call him if he could be of any help to them.

Sunday, two weeks later, the cousins were in church. They waited close by while the pastor was greeting people after the worship service. He realized they wanted to talk to him. They told him that their uncle, who lived in the same town, had died. The pastor expressed his sorrow. The girls confessed they didn't even know their uncle. He was an eccentric painter who left home after high school and never saw his family again. He'd never married; he lived alone. The girls' fathers wanted them to find a pastor in town to do a graveside service. The pastor agreed to conduct the service.

At the graveside, the two students were present with each of their parents. Each father was a brother to the dead man. After the graveside service, the parents insisted the pastor eat lunch with them. They thanked the pastor for the interest he was showing in their daughters. During the meal, the two fathers told their daughters that they would give them a hundred dollars each if they would clean out the deceased man's apartment. If they could sell anything, it would be theirs. He left some expensive paint brushes and paints. He left several finished paintings and many unfinished ones. If they only knew who had bought his paintings in the past they might make a couple of thousand dollars, but they would be lucky if they could sell them at all. But the apartment had stacks of books and magazines that needed to be hauled off. The fathers didn't want to take a day off work to haul off the trash. They were glad to pay their daughters to do it.

The girls agreed to help out their fathers. They would have everything in boxes and trash bags by the weekend. The pastor offered to help. He had a pick-up truck and he'd get a retired deacon who also had a pick-up. They could haul everything away on Monday. The girls said they only had morning classes on Monday. The pastor scheduled to meet them at the dead man's apartment on Monday at 1:00 p.m.

The pastor and the deacon arrived together Monday afternoon. They climbed two flights of stairs to a two-bedroom apartment. The girls greeted them and thanked them for coming to help. Then they started criticizing the place.

Jean asked, "How could a painter who worked with such beautiful colors live in such a dull apartment?"

Jane responded, "How could he paint the beauties of nature and live in such ugliness?

Then Jean, "How could his painting show such order, yet he lived in the midst of trash?"

Jane said, "I'll be glad to get out of this dump. I wouldn't spend a night in this place, even if someone paid me. The door doesn't even lock!"

Jean said, "Except for his paint brushes and paints, there is nothing worth stealing."

Jane said, "All this dust is getting to my allergies. I'll be glad to get out of here."

The girls said they would take to their apartment the box with the paints and paintbrushes and another box with the finished paintings. Everything else could be taken to the trash. It was nothing but trash. They kept saying, "Nothing but trash, trash, trash and more trash!"

The pastor, deacon, and girls started taking boxes and trash bags down the stairs. The girls complained that they were glad to be taking stuff down stairs because they would hate to climb the stairs with that junk.

Jane began to sniffle with her allergies. After everything was on the trucks, they took a break to drink some soft drinks. Jane asked Jean, "I saw a box of Kleenex. Where did you put it?"

Jean answered, "It is on the window sill."

Jane went to the window, got a Kleenex, blew her nose. Then she let out a scream of horror. She grabbed the Kleenex box and sat down on the floor. Everyone jumped up and started toward Jane. A look of terror was on her face. She pointed to the open door and shouted, "The door, the door, the door is open, close it!"

Jean kept going toward Jane, but she kept shouting, "Close the door!"

The deacon closed the door; everyone else went to Jane. They saw in the Kleenex box stacks of 100 dollar bills. They counted the money and it came to $14,000. A Kleenex had covered the money.

The girls said together, "There could be more money in the stuff on the truck!"

Jean said, "Anyone who passes by could pick it up and carry it off! We've got to bring it back up, and quickly."

The girls, who had complained about the weight of taking a single box down the stairs, insisted they could carry two boxes at a time up the stairs.

After everything had been carried up the stairs, the first box of books was opened. Each person took a book and started thumbing through the pages. Jane said, "Well, I guess there is nothing here."

Then the deacon said, "I've found two bills, each a hundred dollar bill."

Before the stores closed, the deacon bought a dead bolt lock and put it on the door. The girls said they'd spend the night in the apartment. They were afraid someone would know of their uncle's hidden treasures and would try to come in to steal them. One went home to get a change of clothes while the other stayed to protect the property.

The pastor and the deacon went home. The two young ladies stayed in the apartment. They called their fathers. The next morning, the deacon returned with his wife, and his daughter, who was a stay-at-home mom. Around 9:30, the two girls' parents showed up. Three days later, every page of every book had been examined. Every possible hiding place was checked out. Thirty-two thousand and four hundred dollars had been discovered. Every single bill discovered was a hundred dollar bill.

The young ladies decided to move into their uncle's place and keep all his furniture. They might find more hidden money. Never did two college students keep an apartment as clean as those two. They were always cleaning and searching for places money could be hidden. In the next twelve months, they found nine hundred more dollars.

DISCUSSION

1. A person's attitude toward a task makes it harder or easier.

2. There is a difference in the attitude of a person who is reluctantly doing a job that must be done and the person doing a job with the expectation of discovering some hidden treasure.

3. The person, who at death leaves only financial treasures, is a very poor person.

CONNECTION TO THE BIBLE

Prov 2:4-5	Seek wisdom as one searches for hidden treasures.
Mt 6:21	Your heart will be where your treasure is.
Lk 15:1-10	The shepherd searched for the lost sheep, and the woman for the lost coin.
1 Cor 15:58	Always give yourselves fully to the Lord's work. Work in the Lord is not in vain.
Col 3:23	Work at whatever you do with all your heart, as working for the Lord, not for people.

HOME WITHOUT A HOUSE

A man and his wife were awakened one night by the piercing scream of the fire alarm. The husband shouted to his wife, "Get out, I'll get our son!"

The house was a total loss with all their furniture and clothes. The family escaped with just the pajamas they were wearing. They stood barefoot on the sidewalk in their pajamas and watched their house burn down. Neighbors and friends quickly got them some clothes and shoes to wear.

The next day the son was sitting in the family pick-up truck while his parents and family friends searched through the burned house for anything that might have escaped the fire. Every once in a while, they found something and placed it in the back of the pick-up truck.

A kind neighbor stopped by the truck to visit with the boy. She said, "Son, I'm so sorry you lost your home."
The boy answered, "We still got our home. We just don't got no house to put it in!"

DISCUSSION

1. It is important to distinguish between things that are of primary value and must be

protected, and things that are of lesser value and can be replaced or discarded.

2. Home is not a building, it is being with family members who love one another.

CONNECTION TO THE BIBLE

Ps 127:1	Laborers' work is useless unless the Lord builds the house.
Prov 3:33	God blesses the home of the righteous.
Prov 15:16	Better to have little and fear God than have wealth with turmoil.

KNOW WHERE YOU BELONG

John and George were country hick cousins who grew up together in the backwoods of the poorest county in their state. They were best friends from the first grade through high school. After high school, George escaped the backwoods by joining the military. He then went to college on the GI bill. He became a famous lawyer who persuaded jurors with his country sense of humor. John stayed in the backwoods and became a logger.

One day George called his cousin, who had been his best friend when they were growing up. He invited John to visit him. George sent John a train ticket. John went to the train station with his ticket in his shirt pocket. John had never traveled on the train and didn't know how to act.

John noticed a group of passengers who were dressed in fine clothes sitting in the waiting room. John felt that those passengers were his social superiors, and he didn't belong with them. John noticed some people standing by the train tracks. Most had dirty and torn clothes. John sauntered up to them, and thought he was where he belonged.

The train pulled into the station. The door to the waiting room opened and passengers from the waiting room boarded the train. The men standing by the train tracks, walked toward the end of the train, and John followed. The train whistle blew and the train began to move. The men ran and jumped into a baggage car with an unlocked door. John also ran and jumped aboard. John noticed that the men moved the baggage and sat or laid down so they couldn't be seen from the door of the baggage car. John also hid behind some baggage. He felt his shirt pocket to make sure the ticket remained in place. John thought he was where he belonged.

The baggage car door opened and a porter accompanied by two policemen entered the baggage car. The three used flashlights to inspect the baggage car and they discovered John and his companions.

The porter asked the hidden passengers, "Tickets please."

John immediately removed the ticket from his shirt pocket and gave it to the porter.

The porter said, "Sir, you have a first class ticket. What are you doing hiding in the baggage car?"

John replied, "I thought this was where I belonged."

The porter said, "When you've got a first class ticket, you should act first class and not like a tramp."

DISCUSSION

1. It's important for people to be conscious of who they are and to be aware of the privileges they deserve.

2. Christ paid the price for believers in him to have a first-class ticket to heaven.

3. The actions of the person who knows who he is will help him receive the respect he deserves.

CONNECTION TO THE BIBLE

Rom 8:16-18, 37	Believers in Jesus are co-heirs with Jesus Christ. They are more than conquerors through Christ who loved them.
2 Cor 4:7	Believers are treasures in jars of clay.
Gal 3:26, 4:7	Believers in Jesus are sons of God.
1 Jn 3:1	God the Father calls those who believe in Jesus "Sons of God."

KNOWN BY FRIENDS

Mr. Farmer kept a few horses. He didn't make money off his horses, but he had fun taking his grandchildren and their friends on trail rides. Mr. Farmer didn't buy expensive registered horses, but he had the ability to choose good riding horses that were obedient and good with children. He was on the lookout for another horse.

One day, Mr. Farmer and his neighbor were working together on the fence that separated their two farms. The neighbor mentioned, "Bought me a horse for my daughter, but she'd rather help her mama in the kitchen than ride a horse. Gonna have to sell it. Could you use another horse?"

Mr. Farmer answered, "Yeah, I could. Let me take your horse home tonight and try him out tomorrow."

Neighbor answered, "Fine with me."

Mr. Farmer connected a rope to the horse's halter and led it to his farm. He set the horse free in the pasture where he kept his horses. The horse held its head up as he walked around looking over the other horses. Then he walked up and greeted each one.

The next morning Mr. Farmer noticed that his neighbor's horse had spent the night sleeping between his two laziest horses. Mr. Farmer said, "Hum. I know you by the friends you've chosen."

Mr. Farmer led the horse back to his neighbor and told him, "This horse is not what I'm looking for. He won't meet my needs."

DISCUSSION

1. The choice of one's friends reveals a lot about one's character.

CONNECTION TO THE BIBLE

2 Chr 19:2	King Jehoshaphat was condemned by God because of his association with King Ahab, the ungodly king of Israel.
Prov 28:7	The person who associates with the riotous brings shame to his parents.
1 Cor 15:33	Evil companions corrupt good morals.

LITTLE GOOD DEED

The slump in the housing market resulted in a cabinet maker closing his shop until construction jobs returned. He advertised himself as a handyman: "No job too small or too big."

The week before school was out for the summer, a customer phoned and asked the handyman to paint a small wooden flat-bottom Jon boat for him. The boat was at their cabin on the lake. He wanted the boat painted before the family arrived for summer vacation.

The handyman picked a clear, dry day when the temperature was predicted to be in the high 70's. He drove to the cabin and found the boat. He used 120-grit sandpaper and a palm sander to sand the surface smooth. While sanding, he noticed a small hole in the bottom of the boat. He got some epoxy from his truck, filled the hole and sanded the area again. He used an oil-based paint. He used a foam brush to paint the wood boat with its first coating. Then he waited a couple of hours until the paint was dry and he applied the second thin coat.

The job took less than a day, but for the unemployed cabinet-maker-turned-handyman, no job was too small. He called the customer and told him the cost of the paint and his fee for a day's work. The handyman received a check in the mail.

The next week the customer came to the handyman's home and offered him a large check.

The handyman said, "You've already paid me for painting your boat."

The customer replied, "This isn't for painting my boat; it's for filling the hole in the bottom."

The handyman said, "That hole took such a little bit of epoxy and such a short time; I didn't charge you for it. You're paying me too much for such a little job."

The customer answered, "My friend, let me tell you what happened. I asked you to paint the boat, but I forgot to mention the hole. It was a small hole. I never expected you to find it. I'd bought some epoxy to fill the hole. When we arrived at the cabin, I got busy helping my wife clean the cabin.

"I went outside to check on the children and discovered they'd put the boat into the water and were out of sight. I remembered that the last time we used the boat it took an hour for water to fill up the boat from that little hole. I was desperate. You can't imagine my relief when I saw them returning safe and sound. I examined the boat and saw where you fixed that hole. I didn't tell you about the hole. Don't you see what you did? You saved the lives of my children! I don't have enough money to pay you for your little good deed."

DISCUSSION

1. A person should take the initiative to do his best when working.

2. Solving small problems may prevent future tragedy.

3. Something small may make a big difference.

CONNECTION TO THE BIBLE

Mt 20:28	Jesus came to serve.
Mk 10:43	In the Kingdom of God, the one who serves is the greatest.
Gal 6:10	When you have the opportunity, do good to all.
Eph 6:5-8	Do your job as if you were serving the Lord.

LOST KEYS

It was a dark night in the parking lot of a large shopping center. Stores had closed. The last show at the theater had just ended. People going to their cars saw a man on his knees, under a lamppost, looking for something on the ground. People who saw the man thought, "At least he lost something under the lamppost. If he'd lost it anywhere else, he would never find it."

One concerned couple asked the man, "Did you lose something?"

The man answered, "Yeah, I dropped my key chain. It's got the keys to my car and house."

The concerned couple realized that after the theater goers left the parking lot, the man would be alone. So they stopped to help. They looked for the lost key chain. Others stopped to help. The couple suggested everyone hold hands and walk back and forth, so they would not leave an area unsearched. The keys weren't found.

The couple asked many questions, "How many keys were on the chain? Were the keys small or large? Were the keys shinny so they would reflect light? Finally they asked the question, "Are you sure you lost the keys under this lamppost?"

The man calmly answered, "No. It was under that lamppost with the burnt-out lamp. But, I couldn't see anything in the dark. However, under this light, I can see much better."

DISCUSSION

1. It is important to search in the right place for what you are looking for.

2. The easiest approach to solving a problem may not be the most productive.

CONNECTION TO THE BIBLE

Gen 13:5-12	Lot looked for prosperity in Sodom.
Mt 7:13-14	Jesus said the wide gate and broad road lead to destruction, while the narrow gate and narrow road leads to life.

LUCK ISN'T TALENT

Once upon a time, a king ordered a jewelry maker to make a ring of gold about the size of a man's fist, and cover it with precious stones. The king ordered his soldiers to put the ring on top of a tall post. Then the king issued a proclamation, "The archer who shoots an arrow through the center of the ring receives the ring as a prize plus a sack of gold."

A thousand archers gathered to aim at the center of the ring. Each shot an arrow. Each missed the target.

A young father was playing with his children close to where the competition was taking place. The young father was teaching his son to shoot a bow and arrow. His son asked, "Daddy, how high can you make an arrow go?"

So the young father pulled the bow string back as far as he could and shot an arrow up into the sky. A sudden gust of wind diverted the direction of the arrow and it went through the center of the ring. The king invited the young father to the palace and rewarded him with the ring and the sack of gold.

The young father left the palace. As he walked through the court yard, he threw his bow and arrow into a fire.

Men gathered around the fire asked, "Why did you throw your bow and arrow into the fire?"

The young father answered, "I had a stroke of good luck; I'd be a fool to think that I have talent with a bow and arrow. Luck isn't talent!"

DISCUSSION

1. A person needs to be aware of talents and skill that contribute to accomplishment, and to accomplishments that are only the results of being in the right place at the right time.

2. Each person should know not only his weaknesses, but also his strengths.

CONNECTION TO THE BIBLE

2 Chr 18:33	King Ahab was killed when someone drew his bow at random and shot an arrow.
Prov 29:23	Pride brings a person down; humility brings one honor.
Mt 23:12	The person who exalts himself will be brought low.
Gal 6:3	The person who thinks himself important when he is nothing, deceives himself.
Rom 12:3	Do not have too high of an opinion of yourself.

MOST IMPORTANT THING

In the early 1800's, two brothers left the coastal State of Virginia and went west to seek their fortunes. One became a rancher in Texas, the other a rancher in Colorado. Both increased the land they owned until each had a large ranch.

The brother in Texas had a beautiful daughter. She fell in love with the son of a neighboring rancher. One day the Texas rancher sent for the young man and said, "I need to send a sack of gold to my brother in Colorado. I need a messenger I can trust."

The young man answered, "You can trust me."

The Texas rancher gave the young man a letter to his brother, a saddle bag with the sack of gold, spending money for his trip and provided him with his best horse. The rancher told the young man, "Protect the most important thing. Take the gold to my brother and good luck."

The confident young man set out early the next morning. He expected success and was unaware of potential problems. He would prove his trustworthiness to the rancher. Then he would ask the rancher for his daughter's hand in marriage. The young man was in a hurry to fulfill his mission. He raced his horse hard. When he passed through small towns, he'd leap from his horse, run into a café, and tell them he was in a hurry to eat. He didn't take time to loosen the horse's saddle. He didn't give the horse time to eat grain or drink water. Several times someone told him, "You're pushing your horse too hard."

The young man answered, "I'm in a hurry. If this horse dies, I'll buy another."

The young man kept pushing the horse. The young man and the horse reached the desolate land of New Mexico, land between Texas and Colorado. Heat was intense. The exhausted horse went slower and slower. Then the horse dropped dead. The young man cursed his bad luck. He removed his saddle and saddle bags from the dead horse and started walking. He remembered the rancher's words, "Protect the most important thing." He put the gold from the saddle bag into his pockets.

It was a long way between ranches in that part of New Mexico. The young man became exhausted; he remembered the rancher's words, "Protect the most important thing." He removed the gold and letter from his pockets and hid them in his boots. He abandoned the saddle and saddle bags and continued walking until he fell exhausted to the ground.

A wagon train of pioneers moving west found the unconscious young man and put him into a covered wagon. Ladies fed and nursed the young man as they traveled. The young man recovered. The wagon train passed close to the Colorado ranch that was the destination of the young man.

The wagon train dropped the young man off at the Colorado ranch.

The young man gave the Colorado rancher the sack of gold and letter. He told him, "Your brother in Texas told me to protect the most important thing. Here's the gold. It's all there."

The Colorado rancher read the letter, "Brother, my daughter wants to marry this young man. I sent him to you as a test. I gave him a sack of gold for you and my best horse. I told him to protect the most important thing. Do me a favor and check out the horse. If he took care of the horse, I'll know he appreciates one who faithfully serves him on his journey. If he abused the animal, I'll know he's only interested in my wealth and wouldn't take care of my daughter nor my employees.

DISCUSSION

1. It is wise to test a person before trusting him.

2. A person's priorities will influence the choices he makes.

3. The things that some people value leads them to disastrous consequences.

4. Our priorities should be the two things that God will never destroy: God's Word and people.

CONNECTION TO THE BIBLE

Prov 12:10	Righteous people take care of their animals.
Mt 6:33	Seek in first place God's Kingdom and his righteousness.
Col 3:1-3	Set your hearts and minds on things above instead of things on earth.

PARACHUTE RIGGER

Crashes of military planes are commonplace. Pentagon records show that the Air Force experiences crashes at the rate of about one every ten days. But there is nothing commonplace about a crash to the pilot who experiences it.

Captain Murphy dreamed about flying before he entered the first grade. All through school, he dreamed of being a pilot. He graduated from the university, joined the Air Force, became a pilot, and then an instructor. Captain Murphy was an F-16 instructor at Luke Air Force Base in Glendale, Arizona.

Captain Murphy was in one F-16; a student pilot was in another F-16 and they were conducting simulated air-to-air combat. Captain Murphy was taking his plane out of a dive when suddenly he felt an explosion in the lone jet engine of his F-16. Captain Murphy had no time to think. Training took over. He leveled his plane, verified the directions of towns and buildings and pointed his plane toward farmland. He reached down between his knees and grabbed and pulled the handle of his ejection seat. The canopy separated from the plane with a loud BANG! A rocket motor exploded, propelling Murphy, still in his seat, 320 yards above his plane. The force of his ejection was in excess of 12 Gs; the force of gravity twelve times his body weight. He felt pressure compacting every muscle in his body. A few seconds after ejecting, his seat automatically deployed his parachute. Captain Murphy then released his seat so he could better control his landing. His parachute was omni-directional. He couldn't control where he went; he was at the mercy of the wind.

As Captain Murphy parachuted down, he observed his F-16 crashing into a distant cornfield. Then Captain Murphy became aware of feeling every muscle in his body; and all the organs insides of his body. He watched the ground below to see where he was heading. He realized, "I'm alive; I'm not dead; God, don't let me break my legs; I'm alive, I'm alive; don't let me break a leg; I'm alive; I've still got a life ahead of me; God, please don't let me break a leg."

The purpose of an ejection seat is pilot survival, not pilot comfort. Many pilots suffer career-ending injuries while using ejection seats. However, Captain Murphy had no injuries beyond bruises and sore muscles all over his body.

Murphy didn't sleep that night. He lay awake in his bed and realized, "I'm fortunate to be alive. I'm fortunate to be able to continue flying. I'm fortunate to continue the life I love." Then he realized that if he had died, no one would miss him except his mother, father, and sister. His niece and nephew wouldn't have missed him. He only saw them at his parents' home at Christmas, and once every summer. He gave them expensive presents, but never did anything special with them. Captain

Murphy lived in the bachelor quarters provided by the Air Force. He lived the "me life." He lived for doing the things that he enjoyed: flying, hunting deer and elk, fishing, hiking, rafting, and canoeing. His near encounter with death made Murphy aware of his need to have other significant people in his life who would also miss him when he died.

The next weekend, Murphy surprised his parents with a visit. The following weekend he surprised his sister with a visit, and he took his niece and nephew fishing. Then Murphy starting searching for a soul mate to become his wife and the future mother of his children.

The first young lady Murphy dated was Molly, the professional model. Murphy thought, "Wow, Molly would make a trophy wife. If I marry Molly, my fellow officers will be envious of my having such a beautiful wife." In the car on the way to the restaurant, Molly's cell phone rang three times and she answered it each time. While they were eating at the restaurant, her cell phone rang five times. She talked on her phone while Murphy stared at the ball game on the big screen TV. Molly lied to some guy named Philip, telling him she was at the gym.

Murphy realized, "It's enjoyable looking at Molly, but it wouldn't be enjoyable living with Molly."

That was the captain's first and last date with Molly.

The second young lady Murphy dated was Sondra, the musician. Sondra played the guitar and sang every weekend at a night club. Murphy thought, "Sondra would make a trophy wife. It would be fun to take her to the officers' club and to parties. She'd be the life of the party as she plays her guitar and sings."

Sondra prided herself on being tolerant. Yet, when Murphy mentioned hunting and fishing, she said, "I can't imagine why anyone would own guns, except for criminals. It's cruel and inhuman to shoot animals or to hook fish."

Murphy thought, "Yeah, it'd be fun to take Sondra to the officers' club, but it wouldn't be fun going home with Sondra."

That was Murphy's first and last date with Sondra.

The third young lady that Murphy dated was Rosa, the marathon runner. She had gorgeous legs. Murphy thought, "Rosa would definitely make a trophy wife. Men would gaze at her and be envious of me."

However, Rosa insisted they go to a restaurant with a self service salad bar. She said, "I'm in training and have to watch what I eat." After eating, Rosa said, "Well, I need to go home. Tomorrow morning at five a.m., I'm meeting other marathon runners for a twelve mile run. I must stretch for forty-five minutes before an intense run. I need my rest. I'm in training."

Murphy realized, "It's enjoyable looking at Rosa, but it wouldn't be enjoyable living with Rosa."

That was the captain's first and last date with Rosa.

The fourth young lady Murphy dated was Jennifer. An officer's wife arranged for Murphy and Jennifer to meet on a blind date. Jennifer had a master's degree in English and taught at a community college. Murphy arrived at her address and discovered that Jennifer drove a pickup truck, lived in a trailer on a 25 acre farm where she raised and trained quarter horses. As soon as he saw her, Murphy realized, "Jennifer will not make a trophy wife! With her figure, she wouldn't even be a consolation prize."

Jennifer was 5'8", and muscular from wrestling hundred pound hay bales to feed the horses. Jennifer's hands were calloused from farm work. Before they headed to a restaurant, Jennifer introduced Murphy to her quarter horses. As soon as they got into Murphy's car, Jennifer opened her cell phone and turned it off.

They arrived at the restaurant and Murphy observed another couple getting out of a shinny Ford F 350 diesel pickup truck. The woman was dressed up, but the man was wearing scratched work boots, torn blue jeans, and a sleeveless red tee shirt. His head was shaved, and his muscular arms were covered with tattoos.

While they were eating, Murphy noticed that Jennifer was nervous. He asked her, "Is something wrong?"

Jennifer replied, "That strange looking man keeps staring at us. He's making me nervous, and – and he's coming toward our table!"

Murphy stood up, ready to defend Jennifer and himself. The man walked up and asked, "Ain't you Captain Murphy?"

Murphy replied, "Yes. Uh, yes, I am."

The man stated, "Then yo' be the captain that bailed out of the F-16?"

Murphy answered, "Uh, yes, but how did you know?"

The man answered, "Oh, I seen yo' picture on TV. I followed the story cause I be the rigger that packed yo' parachute. Well, glad it worked."

Murphy replied. "Oh yes, it worked. If it hadn't worked, I wouldn't be here talking with you. I'm indebted to you."

The man explained, "I be a rigger with the National Guard's Parachute Packing and Maintenance Shop. Spent one weekend a month playing soldier at Camp Mabry. I be the rigger who packs all them parachutes for Luke Air Force Base."

Murphy placed his right hand on the rigger's shoulder and said, "I'm indebted to you. You saved my life."

The man replied, "Ah, just doing my job. If a rigger don't do his job, government calls him a murderer."

Captain Murphy didn't sleep that night, thinking about the Guardsman rigger who had packed his parachute. Murphy thought of the hours the rigger spent on a fifty foot long wooden table inside of a warehouse, carefully weaving the shrouds and folding the silks of each chute, holding in his hands the destiny of someone he didn't know. Murphy realized that if he had run into the rigger while on duty, he wouldn't have spoken to him. He never would have eaten at the same table with the man. Murphy considered himself as the elite; he was an officer; he was a pilot. He would've judged the rigger as being only "support." The rigger wasn't an officer, he wasn't even regular army. He was a Guardsman, a weekend soldier. Yes, he would've considered the Guardsman his inferior.

When Captain Murphy spotted the man getting out of a F-350 pickup with his scratched work boots, torn blue jeans, sleeveless red shirt, shaved head, and tattooed muscular arms, the captain judged him as being his social inferior. Yet, the man he judged as his inferior had packed the parachute that saved his life.

Murphy also realized that he had judged Jennifer inferior to other women, because she wouldn't be a trophy wife. She didn't even have the figure of a consolation prize. But of the ladies he had dated, she would make the best wife. While she wasn't a striking beauty, her eyes showed an excitement for life. She'd turned off her cell phone and given him her undivided attention. If she treats her future husband as well as she treats her horses, it would be a joy coming home to Jennifer.

Murphy decided that his first date with Jennifer would not be his last.

DISCUSSION

1. What guidelines does our culture use to classify someone as either elite or inferior?

2. What guidelines do you use to classify someone as either elite or inferior?

3. In God's Kingdom, servers are superior to takers; those in support are superior to those in leadership.

4. Are there people who serve you either physically, socially, emotionally, or spiritually; however, you've judged them as being your inferiors, yet they've packed some parachutes that enable you to live the life you are living?

5. Are you packing with care the parachute for someone who may judge you as being their inferior? Are you imitating Jesus, doing your best to serve them, even though they will never recognize you and will never tell you, "Thank you"?

CONNECTION TO THE BIBLE

Lk 7:24-28	John the Baptist wore coarse clothes and he preached in the countryside. Temple priests wore fine clothes and lived luxuriously. Jesus said John was the greatest man who had ever lived.

Mt 20:20-28	John and James wanted positions of importance in Jesus' kingdom. Jesus told his disciples that high officials exercise authority over their followers, but the person who wants to become great among his disciples must become a servant. Jesus stated that he didn't come to be served but to serve.
Mk 9:30-37	Jesus' disciples argued about who was the greatest. Jesus told them that if anyone wants to be first, he must be the servant of all.
Jn 13:1-5	The night before Jesus was crucified, he washed his disciples' feet and he told them that he was setting an example for them to follow.
Rom 12:16	Don't be proud. Willingly associate with people of low positions.
Phil 2:5-8	Christians should have the same attitude as Jesus, who was God but made himself nothing and took the nature of a servant.

PRIDEFUL BUCK DEER

It was bow season, the time of year when deer hunters hunted with bow and arrows, but guns were prohibited.

Buck Deer ran through the pastures, jumped fences and ran through the woods. Buck Deer became thirsty and searched for water. He found a creek with a pool of water that was as clear as crystal. Buck Deer lowered his head to drink cool fresh water. He saw his reflection in the water and was proud of his head adorned with antlers that branched out to form points. Then Buck Deer was shocked when he observed the reflection of his skinny crooked legs.

Buck Deer thought about the contrast between the elegance of his head and the ugliness of his legs. Buck Deer thought, "It's true what people say about me. I do look like royalty when I raise my elegant head adorned with a crown of antlers. However, in contrast my skinny crooked legs look horrible."

Buck Deer considered the contrast between his beautiful head and his ugly legs. Meanwhile, a hunter with bow and arrows slipped silently through the woods. Buck Deer heard the snap of a twig as the hunter approached. Immediately, Buck Deer jumped. With two leaps, he was beyond the reach of the hunter's arrow.

Buck Deer ran through the woods. He passed through dense growth of bushes with tangled branches interlocked. Buck's antlers became caught in the tangled branches of bushes. He fought desperately to free his antlers, but in vain. Buck made a lot of racket shaking the bushes in order to untangle his antlers from the branches. The noise guided the hunter to where Buck was trapped. The hunter had no compassion and shot Buck Deer with his arrow.

It's a fact: the legs that Buck so despised were saving his life while the antlers that he prided entrapped him and cost him his life.

DISCUSSION

1. The things that a person most prides about himself may entrap him.

2. People may not give recognition to strengths that are not glamorous.

CONNECTION TO THE BIBLE

Prov 8:13	God hates pride and arrogance.
Prov 11:12	Pride results in disgrace.
Prov 16:18	Pride results in destruction.
Dan 4:37	God is able to humble the proud.
EXAMPLES: PRIDE RESULTING IN DESTRUCTION
Ex 15:4	Pharaoh

2 Sam 14:25-27; 18:9	David's son Absalom cut his hair once a year. Absalom rebelled against his father David. He rode his mule under the thick branches of a oak tree and his hair got caught in the branches.
2 Chr 32:21	Sennacherib
Est 7:9	Haman
Dan 4:33	Nebuchadnezzar
Dan 5:28	Belshazzar

RABBIT'S THESIS

One day Rabbit left his den with some books and a computer. He put his books on a log and his computer on a tree trunk. He got hard at work typing away on his keyboard.

Along came Fox. He eyed Rabbit hard at work. His mouth watered at the idea of a tasty rabbit dinner. But Fox was curious about what Rabbit was doing. Fox slipped up to Rabbit and asked, "Rabbit, what are you doing?"

Rabbit kept typing on his computer, but answered, "I'm working on my doctoral thesis for the university."

Fox asked, "What's the theme of your thesis?"

Rabbit answered, "I'm proving my theory that rabbits are natural predators of foxes."

Fox answered, "That's ridiculous. Everyone knows that Fox Family is the natural predator of rabbits."

Rabbit challenged, "Come with me to my lab which is inside my den. I'll show you the results of my experiments."

Rabbit hopped and Fox trotted to Rabbit's den. Fox was delighted at his fortune. He hoped that Rabbit's parents, brothers, and sisters would be home. Then he could offer a rabbit banquet to family and friends. Rabbit told Fox, "You first." Suddenly, there was a loud ruckus, the noise of teeth chewing on bones, then silence. After a short time, Rabbit returned alone to the tree trunk and went to work typing on his thesis, as though nothing had happened.

About an hour later, Wolf passed by and saw Rabbit hard at work. His first reaction was to give thanks for his lunch. But he was also curious at what held Rabbit's attention. He thought, "I'll find out what Rabbit is doing before I have him for lunch."

Wolf asked Rabbit, "Rabbit, what are you doing?"

Rabbit kept typing on his computer, but answered, "I'm working on my doctoral thesis for the university."

Wolf asked, "What's the theme of your thesis?"

Rabbit answered, "I'm proving my theory that rabbits are natural predators of wolves."

Wolf answered, "That's ridiculous you tasty rabbit. You're off your rocker. Everyone knows that Wolf Family is the natural predator of rabbits."

Rabbit challenged, "Come with me to my lab which is inside my den and I'll show you the results of my experiments."

Wolf couldn't believe his good luck. Rabbit lived in a den with his parents, brothers, and sisters. Wolf thought, "I'll have enough rabbits to share with my family."

Rabbit hopped and Wolf trotted to Rabbit's den. Rabbit told Wolf, "You first." Suddenly, there was a loud ruckus, the noise of teeth chewing on bones, then silence. Then Rabbit again returned alone to the tree trunk and went to work on his thesis, as though nothing had happened.

Inside Rabbit's den was a pile of bones that had once belonged to Fox. On the other side of the room was a pile of bones that once belonged to Wolf. Between the piles of bones was an enormous well fed lion who was picking his teeth.

Lion shortly joined Rabbit. Lion told Rabbit, "I told you. Doesn't matter how ridiculous the theme of your thesis; doesn't matter if your thesis lacks scientific evidence; doesn't matter if your experiments never prove your thesis; doesn't matter if your thesis goes against obvious logic; what matters is who is approving your thesis."

DISCUSSION

1. False teachers will make ridiculous claims that are contrary to the truth.

2. The person who makes the most ridiculous proclamations will find arguments to support his opinions and an authority figure to support his ideas.

CONNECTION TO THE BIBLE

1 Kin 12:31	Anyone could be a priest of the false religion that Jeroboam inaugurated in Israel.
1 Tim 1:7	False teachers don't understand what they are talking about or what they so confidently teach.
1 Tim 4:2	In the last days, some will follow deceiving teachings of hypocritical liars.
2 Tim 4:3	The time will come when people will not put up with sound teaching.
2 Pet 2:1	False teachers will introduce destructive heresies that will bring destruction on themselves and bring the way of the truth into disrepute.

REVENGE DESIRES

One day nine year old Billy came home from school. Billy's father was in the back yard working in their small garden. Billy threw his backpack on the floor, stormed out the back door, and slammed the door. Then he sulked out into the back yard, kicked the fence, and then he kicked the dog.

Billy's father asked, "Billy, why are you cruel to your dog? What's up?"

Billy answered, "I wish Johnny would break his leg. Then he could never play soccer! I wish he'd get sick and never come back to school again! Johnny embarrassed me in front of my friends. He made my friends laugh at me. I wish something bad would happen to him."

Billy's father marched into the house and got a clean white shirt and hung it on a tree limb. He went to the barbeque grill and got a half-full sack of charcoal. He placed the sack twenty steps from the shirt. He told Billy, "Pretend that shirt is Johnny and each charcoal is something bad you wish to happen to Johnny. Throw each one of these charcoals at the shirt."

Billy's father returned to working in the garden, but kept his eyes on Billy.

Billy thought that would be fun. He picked up one piece of charcoal and shouted, "Break a leg;" another piece of charcoal and, "Get sick;" another piece charcoal and, "Your house burns down;" another and, "Wreck your bike."

The white shirt was 20 steps away and only one in ten pieces of charcoal hit the shirt. Billy emptied the sack of charcoal. Billy's father returned and asked, "How do you feel now?"

Billy answered, "I feel great. Every time I hit the shirt, I felt like I hit Johnny."

Billy's father took him by the hand, led him into the house, and stood him in front of a full length mirror. Billy was covered with smut, except for his eyes and teeth.

Billy's father said, "Son, look at yourself. The white shirt has a few charcoal smut marks but you're covered with smut. When you want revenge, the bad things you wish for someone else dirties you more than the person you hate. Every desire for revenge leaves smut on you. I can make you take a bath to get rid of the smut, but you must clean your thoughts to get rid of smut residue from your desire for revenge."

DISCUSSION

1. The seeker of revenge usually hurts himself more that the person he desires to hurt.

2. God teaches us to do good to those who hurt us instead of seeking revenge.

CONNECTION TO THE BIBLE

Prov 25:21	If your enemy is hungry, feed him; if he is thirsty give him water.
Mt 5:44	Jesus gave guidelines on how to treat your enemies: love them, bless them, do good to them and pray for them.
1 Pet 3:9	Do not repay evil with evil, but pay evil with blessing.
EXAMPLES OF RETURNING GOOD FOR EVIL	
Gen 45:15; 50:20	Joseph forgave and provided for the brothers who had sold him into slavery.
Num 12:1-13	Miriam criticized Moses. Then God punished her with leprosy. Moses prayed for God to heal Miriam.
1 Sam 24:1-19; 26:1-24	King Saul was trying to kill David. Twice, David spared Saul's life.
2 Kin 6:6-22	Elisha spared the lives of soldiers who tried to capture him.
Ac 7:60	Stephen prayed for God to forgive the men who were stoning him.

SOCCER DADDY

Children's soccer leagues should teach children to play by the rules, learn team work, and enjoy playing a sport. However, sometimes organized soccer teaches children that those who play by the rules are called, "Losers."

The Carringtons were soccer parents. Their seven year old son, Shawn, started playing in the U-10 soccer league. All the players on his team were under ten years old when soccer season began. Every Tuesday and Thursday afternoons, Mrs. Carrington took Shawn from school to soccer practice. Every Saturday, Mr. and Mrs. Carrington went to the park to watch Shawn play.

Seven year old Shawn went to every one of his team's practices. He said, "It's not fair. Some nine year olds don't come to practice, yet coach gives them a lot of playing time on Saturday." Coach only let Shawn and the other seven year olds play two minutes each during each game.

Soccer league rules require that each player plays at least one-half of each game. However, the rule is only enforced during tournament weekend at the end of the season. During tournament weekend, an official on the sidelines keeps records to make sure each player plays at least one-half of each game.

When Shawn was nine years old, he was one of the biggest and best players in the under-ten league. He played all the time while seven year old team mates only played two minutes per game.

Shawn turned ten years old and moved up to the under-twelve year old league. Mr. Carrington became his son's coach. The first day that Coach Carrington practiced with his team, the older players told the new coach, "Those younger boys are only two-minute players."

Coach Carrington promised, "I'm going to follow the rule that every player who comes to practice gets to play at least half the game. I know the rule is only enforced during tournament weekend when an official on the sidelines keeps records of each player's playing time, but we're going to play by the rule."

Coach Carrington's team dreaded playing Coach Brute's team. Coach Brute's team had won the last three tournament championship games. He had the best winning record. Coach Brute shouted and hollered at his team. He screamed if the referee penalized one of his players. Coach Brute wanted to win every game. His weaker players only played two minutes per game. If Coach Brute's team were ahead 17 to 0 and the other team scored, Coach Brute would scream at his defensive players for slacking off.

The goal keeper on Coach Carrington's team was named Lee. Coach Carrington and other fathers kicked the ball to Lee during practice to help him prepare for defending the goal against Coach Brute's team.

Saturday came. The two teams entered the soccer field to warm up. Coach Brute shouted, "Boys, we gonna teach that new coach a lesson!"

Coach Carrington started off with his best players to give his team confidence. The teams were evenly matched. Coach Carrington realized his best players were playing as equals to equals with Coach Brute's team. Lee only had to defend the goal twice, because his team mates kept the opposing team away from scouring position. Coach Carrington realized that his team could win if he played by Coach Brute's rule and only gave the weaker players two minute playing time. However, if every player played at least half of the game, there was no way he could win. Coach Carrington began to send in his weaker players half way through the first half. The game took a dramatic turn. Coach Brute's team made its first goal. Coach Brute shouted, "Teach them a lesson; now make another one!"

Lee in quick succession defended the goal three times. His parents and friends were cheering, "Go-Lee; Go-Lee."

Without Coach Carrington's best players, Coach Brute's team was constantly getting into scoring position. Lee was an outstanding athlete, but he was no match for Coach Brute's offensive team. Lee recklessly threw his body in front of incoming balls. Then Coach Brute's team scored two goals in quick succession. Lee became a raging maniac, shouting at his team. He recklessly threw his body onto the ball in front of a player who had pulled back his foot to kick a goal. Lee took the player's kick, and it hurt. Lee then threw the ball to one of his team mates. But one of Coach Brute's players stole the ball. Lee covered the boy with the ball, but that boy kicked it to another boy. By the time Lee repositioned himself, it was too late; Coach Brute's team scored a fourth goal.

After the fourth goal, Lee retrieved the ball from the net and handed it to the referee. Coach Brute saw tears running down Lee's cheek and shouted, "Give the crybaby something to cry about!"

Lee's father stood up and shouted, "Shut up or somebody will give you something to cry about!"
Lee's mother told her husband, "Sit down! You won't help your son by fighting that bully. Now sit down and behave yourself!"

Coach Brute's team made two more goals in quick succession. Then Lee went to his knees, put his fists to his eyes and cried the tears of the helpless and brokenhearted.

Lee went to his knees; his father started onto the field. His wife clutched his arm and said, "Honey, don't. You'll embarrass him." But the father tore loose and ran onto the field. He wasn't supposed to; the game was still in progress. Lee's father picked up his son, took him to the sidelines, held him tight, cried with him and said, "Lee, I'm proud of you. I want everybody to know that you're my son."

Lee sobbed, "Daddy, I couldn't stop them. I tried. Daddy, I tried and tried, but they keep scoring on me."

The father said, "Son, Coach Brute plays by different rules than Coach Carrington. Son, it doesn't matter how many times they score on you. You're my son, and I'm proud of you. You want to quit, but go back out there for Coach Carrington. Don't quit. Son, you're going to get scored on again, but things will be different when tournament weekend comes."

Coach Brute shouted for the referee to expel Lee from the game because his father had invaded the playing field. The referee knew that Coach Brute wasn't playing by the rules and he told Coach Brute, "Shut up or I'll expel you from the game."

Lee ran back on the playing field. He did his best; however, Coach Brute's team repeatedly scored against him. But there was a difference in Lee, the way he held his head up. It made a difference knowing that his father and Coach Carrington considered him a winner, no matter how many times Coach Brute's team scored against him.

Tournament weekend came. During the tournament, an official on the sidelines kept records to make sure each player played at least one-half of each game. The best players could play the entire game, but the coaches had to sub in and out others; so each one played at least one half of each game.

At the final game of tournament weekend, Coach Carrington's and Coach Brute's teams met for the championship game.

During the season, Coach Carrington's weaker players had gained experience from playing one half of each game and had improved. The former two-minute players improved with experience and began to make good plays. They gained confidence. Coach Brute's weaker players had remained two-minute players and remained weak players. Now, Coach Brute was forced to play his two-minute-players for half the game. Coach Brute screamed at his players who were unable to make any goals while Coach Carrington's players made six goals.

Coach Carrington's team won the tournament!

There are times when I'm on a team that is playing by different rules than the other team. I get scored on again and again. I struggle with temptation and sin with every ounce of my being. When I play by the rules of truth and honesty, the opposing team plays by the rules of lies and deceit.

When I play by the rule of purity, the opposing team plays by the rule of lust. When I play by the rule of caring, the opposing team plays by the rule of greed. When I play by the rule of love, the opposing team plays by the rule of hate.

It means a lot to me to know that God, my Father, is proud of me when I'm playing by his rules; even though, people who play by different rules constantly score against me. When I get so desperate after getting scored against that I fall to my knees – defeated, helpless and embarrassed, the Father comforts me with the Holy Spirit.

When I'm playing by God's rules and others consider me a loser, it helps to know that Coach Jesus will greet me as a winner at the end of life's season. Those who play by God's rules may be demoralized, ridiculed, and called losers; but at the end of life's season, the tables will be turned. It'll pay in the end to play by God's rules.

DISCUSSION TOPICS

1. The followers of Jesus live by different rules than people who don't know God.

2. How have you experienced being scored against when you were playing by different rules than others?

3. What inspires you to play by God's rules when others are gaining the advantage by ignoring the rules?

CONNECTION TO THE BIBLE

Ps 73	The psalmist agonized over the defeat of the righteous and the victory of the evil.
Prov 28:5	Evil people do not understand what justice means.
Mt 5:48; 6:8	One theme of the Sermon on the Mount is: Be perfect like the Father; don't be like them.
Mt 6:31-32	Non-believers worry about what they will eat, drink and wear. Jesus' followers seek first the Kingdom of God.
Mt 20:25-28	The world's great desire is to be served; God's great desire is to serve.
Jn 3:19-21	People love darkness because their deeds are evil. Those who love the truth seek the light.
Jn 15:18-19	The world loves those who are of the world, but it hates Jesus' followers.
Jn 16:33	Jesus' followers will have trouble in this world.
1 Jn 2:15-17	The things of the world will pass away, but the person who does the will of God will last forever.

TRAFFIC CAMERA

A man pulled out of a shopping mall. He drove through a green light and he saw the flash of a traffic camera. He figured that his picture had been taken for exceeding the speed limit. The man knew that he was not speeding. He saw a posted sign: Speed Limit, 45 miles per hour. He was only doing 40 miles per hour. Just to be sure, he went around the block a second time and passed the same spot, driving more slowly, doing 35 miles per hour; again the camera flashed.

He smiled and went around the block a third time and passed the same spot driving even more slowly, doing 30 miles per hour; again the camera flashed. Now he was chuckling out loud. He went around the block a fourth time and passed the same spot driving even more slowly, doing 25 miles per hour; again the camera flashed. He was laughing out loud as he drove around the block a fifth time going at a snail's pace of 10 miles per hour.

Two weeks later, he received in the mail five tickets for driving without a seat belt. Attached to each ticket was his picture driving the car without wearing his seat belt!

DISCUSSION

1. A person can think he is right and be completely wrong.

2. Wrong conclusions result in undesirable consequences.

CONNECTION TO THE BIBLE

Prov 3:7	A person should not consider himself to be wise.
Prov 11:2	Pride is followed by shame.
Gal 6:3	The person who thinks himself important when he is nothing, deceives himself.

TRASH OR TREASURE

Bill and Sue went to the beach for a second honeymoon. The children stayed with Sue's parents. Bill and Sue had a good marriage, but were incompatible when it came to their wake-up clocks. When they were on vacation, Bill went to bed early and got up in time to see the sun rise over the ocean. Sue read late into the night and enjoyed sleeping until the morning was half over.

The first morning, Bill slipped out of bed before sunrise and left Sue sleeping. He took a book and sat on a bench in front of the beach. It was too dark to read. Bill watched the eastern sky come alive with colors. Bill noticed he was sharing the same beach with two other early risers.

One of the early risers looked like a homeless wino who had slept on the sandy beach. The wino pushed a grocery cart along the sidewalk going from trash can to trash can. He salvaged the trash and removed cans and bottles. He put glass bottles in one garbage sack, plastic bottles in another, and cans into another. If he found a container with alcohol, he finished it off. He opened snack bags and ate the remaining potato chips, pretzels, and crackers with peanut butter.

The other early riser was pulling a little red wagon filled with a metal detector and accessories. The wagon looked like it belonged to a child instead of a middle aged, pot-bellied man with skinny legs.

Bill observed the man remove a medal detector from the wagon, mark off an area, and then go back and forth over the sand until the detector let out a loud beep-beep-beeping sound. He marked the place and removed a sand scoop and a shifter from the wagon. He scooped sand into the shifter, then shook the shifter and sand fell to the beach while tabs from cans, jewelry and coins remained. The man put trash into a plastic sack and treasures found into a plastic tray.

Bill watched the two men, and he had an insight: Two men were sharing the same beach during the same sunrise; one was looking for trash and the other was looking for treasure, and each found what he was looking for. Bill thought, "As I share space on earth with others, I can either look for trash or search for treasure. And I'll find what I'm looking for."

DISCUSSION

1. A person will see what he focuses on. Where one person focuses on beauty, the other will focus on ugliness.

CONNECTION TO THE BIBLE

| Mt 6:22-23 | Good eyes see light; bad eyes see darkness. |
| Mt 6:33 | Seek first God's Kingdom and righteousness. |

Rom 12:2	Be transformed by the renewing of your minds.
2 Cor 4:18	Fix eyes on the unseen, not on the seen, not the temporary but what is eternal.

USELESS NAILS

Church members worked together to build a new church building. The members completed the church building and scheduled a Dedication Day to celebrate and dedicate the new church building. People came from far and wide to celebrate the accomplishment and to admire the beauty of the new church building.

Comments were heard:
"The stained glass is beautiful."
"The murals are gorgeous."
"The carpet is soft and beautiful."
"The padded benches are well made and comfortable."
"The pulpit furniture was hand crafted. It's a work of art."
"What a beautiful new pulpit Bible."
"The stained wooden beams are strong and beautiful."
"The sound system is fantastic."

The nails that held the ceiling and roof in place heard all the bragging about the beauty of the church, but no one mentioned them.

A ceiling nail complained, "They've covered us with paint. Nobody even knows we are here."

A roofing nail lamented, "We're out of sight and out of mind."

The nails formed a chorus, "We're out of sight, we're out of mind, we're so insignificant, nobody would miss us."

So the nails agreed to stop applying pressure to hold the ceiling and roof in place. That night it rained, and the wind blew. It poured down rain and the winds howled. The nails that had let go of the roof were washed to the ground and the roof was blown away. Water ran down onto the ceiling. Without the nails holding the ceiling in place, the ceiling fell onto the pews. The water ran down the side of the walls and stained the gorgeous murals. The beautiful carpet was spoiled. The pulpit Bible was soaked and its pages warped.

During the cleanup, the nails were swept out of the building into the mud. Mud covered the nails. So again, the nails were out of sight, and they became completely useless. Their destiny was to erode away by rust!

DISCUSSION

1. Unobserved and unrecognized people are important for an organization to work.

2. When people who consider themselves to be insignificant fail to do their jobs, tragedy occurs.

3. There are no insignificant jobs; there are insignificant ways of doing a job.

CONNECTION TO THE BIBLE

Rom 12:3-8	The body of Christ has many members. Each member has his own function and should fulfill it.
1 Cor 12:4-28	There is a diversity of spiritual gifts within the church. People with different gifts are compared to parts of the human body. All are important.

RESTRICTED WATER BUFFALO

My wife and I used to live in Brazil. Once we took a six hour ship ride from the city of Belém to Marajó Island. Marajo is a phenomenal island in the Amazon Delta about 110 miles down river from Belém on the Tocantins River. At night, we slept in hammocks on a church porch.

The Equator passes through Marajó Island. Constant breezes endow it with pleasant temperatures. It is surrounded by the Amazon River on one side, the Tocantins River on the other and it borders the Atlantic Ocean; however, the waters that bathe the island are always fresh. The force of the Amazon's flow pushes ocean salt water more than a hundred miles away from the coast. The island's land mass is the size of Switzerland. It is the largest river island in the world. It was formed by gigantic waves where the waters of the Amazon River met the Atlantic Ocean. The island's few roads are elevated three meters so they will remain above water when the Amazon floods.

Water buffalos, alligators, monkeys, and large anaconda snakes are some of the common animals on Marajó Island. The island has water buffalo ranches. Portuguese settlers brought water buffalo to Brazil from Asia centuries ago. Water buffalos are well adapted to wetland conditions. Water buffalos are useful to farmers: carrying cowboys, pulling carts, pulling plows in wetlands, and providing the ranch with milk and meat.

My wife and I were fascinated to see water buffalo wandering the streets. We saw policemen riding water buffalo. We saw buffalo pulling carts and carrying heavy loads. They can almost carry their own weight. We watched them dive into ponds on hot days and were amazed that they could stay several minutes under water. The water buffalo weighs 1800 - 2600 pounds. It is a massive, powerful animal, with the widest horn span of any animal.

Brazil's army is drafting water buffalo from Marajo Island. They are a low-tech but effective transporter for Amazon military operations. Brazil has some 27 military bases securing its rugged Amazon border, a frontier abutting seven nations that stretches 6,800 miles -- three times the length of the U.S. border with Mexico. The buffalo eats almost any green plants. They don't require special food. Supplies arrive at military bases by plane or boat, then the buffalo transports the supplies along narrow trails in remote jungle areas where there are no roads nor airports, and where rivers are too shallow to navigate.

My wife and I were fascinated to see powerful water buffalos tied to fence posts by strips of leather no thicker than a shoe lace, or by small nylon ropes. After being tied to a small post, a buffalo would stand still, waiting for its master to remove the rope and lead it away. The buffalos could easily have broken the leather strips or ropes that tied them to the post. If the ropes had been strong, the buffalo could have pulled the post out of the ground.

I wondered why those powerful animals did not free themselves. Why did they wait in the hot tropical sun, when they could have broken the cords that held them and wandered to a shaded spot? Why did they remain tied to a small post in the hot sun when they could have been more comfortably bathing in a nearby pool?

I finally realized why the powerful water buffalo didn't free himself from the cords that bind him. When the buffalo was a little calf, the first time a man separated him from his mama and tied him to a post, the calf fought the cord all night. He may have even fought it for a night and a day. Finally he became exhausted, gave up and quit fighting. After that first night, he thought it useless to fight the cord that bound him to a post.

I felt pity for this powerful water buffalo that no longer fights the cord that binds him. I felt pity for this enormous animal that allows a weak cord to bind him. He grew large and strong; however, he allows a weak, small cord to bind him, because he gave up fighting for his freedom.

I thought about people who are like those water buffalos. When they were small and weak, a bigger and stronger person abused them and bound them with emotional cords. When they were small and weak, they were helpless to break those cords. But years have passed; they have become bigger and stronger. Those who bound them have become older and weaker. However, many have never freed themselves from the emotional cords that bound them when they were small and weak. They stopped fighting the emotional cords that bind them. They give into old conditioning and say they can't do anything right, they can't accomplish any goal or resolve any problem. They excuse themselves by claiming their father had an anger problem, so they are hot-headed. They use the excuse that they have addictions to multiple sex partners, or drugs, or alcohol because of their upbringing. They are like those gigantic water buffalos who are restrained by a weak strip of leather.

DISCUSSION

1. Abuses experienced in childhood can bind a person to emotional chains; but with Christ, those chains can be broken.

2. People often don't remember events in their childhood that trigger actions when they are adults.

3. Victims of abusive actions must assume responsibility for choices they make.

4. The Gospel of Jesus enables a person to free himself from sinful habits that bind him.

CONNECTION TO THE BIBLE

Eze 11:19	God promised to take away his people's stony heart and give them a new heart.
2 Cor 5:17	The believer in Jesus is a new creature.
Col 3:5-10	Put to death actions that belong to your sinful nature. Rid yourself of the way you once lived, because you have taken off your old self and put on the new self.

WEIGHED DOWN BY HONOR

A long, long, long time ago before there were guns, soldiers fought wars with bows and arrows. They fought with swords and spears in hand-to-hand combat.

Young Sir Wiley was a brave soldier and a skilled swordsman. Within his army, he won all sword fighting competitions. He received many medals for winning sword fighting competitions. On the battlefield, he defeated every enemy soldier he fought. He received many medals of honor for bravery and heroic action in battle. Fellow soldiers admired him for his skills and courage. Ladies adored him for his strength, good looks, charm, and for being a hero.

After many years of fighting as a soldier, Sir Wiley's uniform was covered with medals for winning sword fighting competitions, and medals of honor for his skill on the battlefield. One afternoon, in the middle of a hard-fought battle, Sir Wiley was wounded by an enemy's sword. Sir Wiley thought, "I'm the best swordsman. Today, I was almost killed, and I'm better than the man who wounded me."

Sir Wiley realized the problem. The weight of the medals on his uniform was slowing him down and hindering his movements. Sir Wiley threw his uniform jacket with all its medals to the ground and returned to battle where he defeated his enemy.

Recognition and honor for past victories shouldn't become a weight that hinders us in present challenges.

DISCUSSION

1. Displaying past accomplishments can hinder a person from facing present challenges.

2. Recognition and honor for past victories shouldn't become a weight that hinders a person in present situations.

CONNECTION TO THE BIBLE

Prov 11:2	Pride is followed by disgrace.
Mt 23:12	The person who exalts himself will be humbled.
Phil 3:4-8	The things that had given Paul pride in the past, he now considered loss for Christ's sake.
Phil 3:12-14	Paul forgot past accomplishments and pressed forward to win the prize for which God had called him.
Heb 12:1-2	The Christian should throw off everything that hinders or entangles him in the spiritual race and run with perseverance.

WHEAT

A man grew up on his father's wheat farm. He finished high school, went to college, and became a school teacher in a large city. He married and had children.

Each summer, the man took his children home to his father's farm so he could help with the wheat harvest. One summer day, the father took his young son for a walk through the golden colored wheat field. The wheat stalks were almost as tall as the little boy.

When wheat is ready for harvest, the heads of the grain start to bend the stalks with the weight of the kernels. This, in combination with the golden color, indicates that it is time to harvest the wheat.

The boy became fascinated with the stalks of wheat. He noticed some were tall and straight; others were bent over, almost touching the ground. The boy said, "Daddy, some of the stalks of wheat stand straight and others lean over, almost touching the ground. Are the stalks that stand up straight the good, strong ones, and are the ones that lean over the bad, weak ones?"

The father replied, "Son, the stalks that are leaning over are full of good wheat grain. The heads of the grain bend the stalks with the weight of the kernels. The ones that are proudly standing tall are full of dried up kernels, and they are no good."

DISCUSSION

1. Often the one who stands tall has nothing to brag about.

2. First impressions may be wrong. The person who makes the first impression of being useless may become the most useful. The person who first appears useful may become the most useless.

3. It is more important to bear fruit than to give a good show.

CONNECTION TO THE BIBLE

Ps 18:27	God saves the humble and brings down the haughty.
Prov 29:23	The prideful will be brought low and the humble upheld.
Dan 4:29-34	When King Nebuchadnezzar boasted with pride, he was reduced to living like an animal.
Mal 4:1	The day will come when the proud will be burned as though they were stubble.
Mt 7:16	People will be known by what they produce.

Mt 19:29-30	Many who are considered first will be last, and many who are considered last will be first.
Mt 23:12	The person who humbles himself will be honored, the person who honors himself will be humbled.
Lk 1:51-52	Mary sang that God had scattered the proud, brought down rulers and lifted up the humble.
Lk 16:19-31	Parable of the Rich Man and Lazarus